T0277727

Nevermore

THE FRENCH LIST

Nevermore

CÉCILE WAJSBROT

TRANSLATED BY
TESS LEWIS

LONDON NEW YORK CALCUTTA

PAP
TAGORE

The work is published with the support of the
Publication Assistance Programmes of the Institut français

Seagull Books, 2024

First published in French as Cécile Wajsbrot, *Nevermore*

First published in English translation by Seagull Books, 2024

ISBN 978 1 80309 389 5

British Library Cataloguing-in-Publication Data
A catalogue record for this book is available from the British Library

Typeset at Seagull Books, Calcutta, India
Printed and bound in the USA by Integrated Books International

CONTENTS

PRELUDE

'Well, we must wait for the future to show,' said Mr. Bankes, coming in from the terrace.

We must wait for the future to appear, said Mr. Bankes, coming in from the terrace. We must wait and see what the future brings, said Mr. Bankes, entering from the terrace. We must wait for the future to show, said Mr. Bankes, as he entered the house from the terrace. We must see what the future has in store, said Mr. Bankes, coming in from the terrace.

Let's see what the future has in store. Let us wait and see what the future . . . Well, we must wait for the future . . . said Mr. Bankes, entering from the terrace.

There once was a woman who wrote. In a large city, a capital, she wrote about a house lost on a coast—a place she had stopped going long before—and she wrote about a lost time, or rather, about the passage of time.

A writer who was trying to capture the moment, as she said, but also trying to capture traces of human presence in eternity.

Trying to capture them in a book called *To the Lighthouse*, a title translated into French as *La Promenade au phare*, the stroll to the lighthouse. The movement of the word *to* is implicit in the word *promenade*. But can you call taking a boat to a lighthouse a stroll? Aren't strolls, by definition, taken on solid ground? Later, there will be other versions of the title. *Voyage au phare*, trip to the lighthouse. *Vers le phare. Au phare*, bound for the lighthouse, toward the lighthouse. All of them run aground somewhat on the obviousness of *to* and are unable to reproduce it. The first German translation is called *Die Fahrt zum Leuchtturm*, the trip to the lighthouse, and a more recent version is *Zum Leuchtturm*, to the lighthouse. German offers more opportunities for a literal translation than French because it can trace the English construction. But this result is compact, the syllables too dense compared to the airy sound of the English title. Perhaps that's why the first translation added *Die Fahrt*, the equivalent of the French *promenade*, but unlike a promenade, *Fahrt* contains the idea of a distance to be covered, one that generally requires some means of transport, which could be a boat or a sailboat. In this sense, *Voyage au phare* would be the most exact with the same number of syllables as the English title and its light, breezy tone. Even if *voyage* or journey seems a bit exaggerated for a simple crossing, an excursion. But didn't this journey last more than ten years? And who can measure the duration of a journey? It begins long before the simple transit and ends long after—if it ever does end . . .

'It's almost too dark to see,' said Andrew coming up from the beach.

Mr. Bankes isn't the only character. Nor is he the main character, any more than Andrew is. Are they even characters at all?

It's almost too dark to see, said Andrew, returning from the beach. There's barely enough light left to see, said Andrew, back from the beach. It's so dark, you can hardly see a thing, said Andrew coming up from the beach.

Too dark, barely enough light, to see, to see a thing. Coming back, back from the beach. *Coming in, coming up*. These postpositions are very tricky. Do I have to translate them exactly? Can I ignore them? They do add something, of course, and this something is an important nuance. But would it be so bad to drop them for the sake of rhythm and repetition? Or to mark the difference in another way? Venant, revenant? Coming up, coming back? And then, too dark to see what—the future?

Night is falling, will fall, they're coming home one after the other.

'One can hardly tell which is the sea and which is the land,' said Prue.

Andrew and Prue are part of the Ramsay family, while Mr. Bankes is a friend. The Ramsay family is at the heart of the novel, or rather the mother, Mrs. Ramsay, is. There are eight children, among them Andrew and Prue, and James, too. He is the youngest, the one who wants to go to the lighthouse and to whom his mother promises they will go although his father says it won't be possible. They would go, his mother tells him, if the weather is fine. But it won't be fine, his father says. James hates his father. All the hatred a child can feel toward his father is concentrated in this exchange, in the question of whether or not it would rain the following day. On the one hand, the mother is giving her son hope and trying to comfort him, on the other, the father is sticking to the facts—you're indulging him with illusions, he chides Mrs. Ramsay, it's obvious that it will rain. And, in fact, it does rain the following day. But for Mrs. Ramsay there are more important things than facts and these are the phenomena that pass like clouds in the children's sky, phenomena that certain adults strive to ignore, no longer knowing how to raise their eyes, how to escape from the weight of the world, those intangible moments of being that Virginia Woolf tries to capture in *To the Lighthouse* and in her other books, as elusive as the translation of that *to* into other languages. *Al faro*, in Spanish. *Al faro* in Italian. Too short. In Italian, the title of the first translation was *Gita al faro*. *Gita*, excursion. The meaning is there, the syllable count too, and yet something is off. The rhythm, maybe. With *Gita*, the accent is on the beginning of the sentence, whereas in English we have to wait until the end for the essential part. We have to wait until we've reached the lighthouse.

'One can hardly tell which is the sea and which is the land,' said Prue.

It is difficult to tell which is the sea and which is the land. One can hardly distinguish the sea from the land or the land from the sea. One can hardly tell where the sea begins and where the land ends.

It is the beginning of time. There was a before, of course, there was day, but everything begins, begins again, at night. Genesis. The beginning of time. "Time Passes," the second part of *To the Lighthouse*, can be read as a separate work, a text we can approach as we would an island from which, to be sure, the contours of the shoreline, of the mainland can be seen—but the only thing that counts is the exploration of the island. A creation story. Dividing light from darkness. Dividing the waters, those above would be the sky, those below the sea. Then there would be the earth. The genesis of *To the Lighthouse* differs slightly from the biblical one. It's night that intrudes on the day and the land can hardly be distinguished from the sea. There is no sky. A recommencement rather than a beginning.

'Do we leave that light burning?' said Lily, as they took their coats off indoors.

'No,' said Prue, 'not if everyone's in.'

Do we leave the light on? Do we leave that light on? said Lily as they took their coats off indoors. Should we leave the light on? said Lily as they were taking off their coats indoors. No, said Prue, not if everyone's in. Do we leave the light burning? said Lily, as they took off their coats. No, said Prue, since everyone's in. And *indoors*? Why not leave it out if "in" comes in the next sentence?

Translation is an inexact science, an attempt that's always doomed—not to failure but to imperfection. In transit from one language to another, the ferryman's boat encounters obstacles that it confronts or skirts, strong waves or gentle swells, quickening currents or countercurrents. Translation is a crossing with a point of departure and a point of arrival, but what lies between the two, the passage with its reefs and shallows, is known by only one person, the one who has passed through every stage.

'Andrew,' she called back, 'just put out the light in the hall.'

Andrew, she called back, turn off the light in the hall. Andrew, she called, put out the light in the hall. Would you put out the light in the hall? The last version is phrased as a question, which does justice somewhat to the *just* by slightly softening the imperative, even if a bit too much. You'll put out the light in the hall? The hall light?

In any case, the light is turned off, night can fall, and the story can begin, begin again. Although not entirely.

One by one the lights were all extinguished, except that Mr. Carmichael, who liked to lie awake a little reading Virgil, kept his candle burning rather longer than the rest.

One after another, the lights were extinguished, except that of Mr. Carmichael, who liked to stay awake a little reading Virgil and kept his candle burning longer than the others. One by one, the lights went out, but Mr. Carmichael, who liked to lie awake for a time reading Virgil, kept his candle lit longer than the others. Or rather: left his lit?

A man keeping watch in the night with Virgil as his guide, for one must be guided on the threshold of the Underworld, and yet, if Mr. Carmichael's candle is kept burning a little longer than the rest, the implication is that it too will be extinguished.

INTERLUDE

Promenade—does this slow, carefree word really suit the way to the footbridge that you arrive at by climbing successive flights of stairs to the elevated track before being able to walk with a sense of security on the polished wood planks while below you parallel streets lead to the Hudson River . . . Gansevoort Street. Peter Gansevoort, a colonel in the Continental Army, who actively participated in the invasion of Quebec, the capture of Montreal, the American Revolutionary War. Names of battles, military ranks—ascent in the hierarchy. But in the end, isn't his greatest honor that he was Melville's grandfather? Is Gansevoort Street, the only one that passes under the High Line with a proper noun instead of a number, in fact, named after him?

Up on the High Line, it's another world; a few meters above the ground, everything is different. The promenade is planted with trees, grasses, and flowers. Plants are the first immigrants: they always come from elsewhere, seeds scattered on the wind, carried on a breeze or in a bird's beak, and sown where they create an impression of distant places, introducing colors and forms and resonant names of other countries. And, whereas everyone on the streets below is caught up in his or her mundane preoccupations, up on the High Line, people stroll, talk, reflect. It offers a glimpse of a different kind of city, a city that has time to make less noise, to resist indulging in rumors—an idealized image. A parenthesis in the tumult, an island off the merciless continent, it offers leisure, an oasis—it offers time.

Do we have any idea, today, of the commotion caused by the arrival of the farmers who set up their stalls, the street vendors, the trucks discharging their goods, fruits and vegetables, poultry, eggs . . . Nights, at four in the morning, cattle were slaughtered in the surrounding buildings and their meat was preserved in refrigerated storage rooms installed early in the twentieth century or consumed in the restaurants on site. Upton Sinclair described the conditions in which cattle were slaughtered in his novel *The Jungle*, which is set in Chicago, but slaughterhouses everywhere are much the same, as are the workers who slave away in them for the sake of inaccessible wealth, which, thanks to credit, they have been led to believe is within their reach. That was in 1905—was the mechanism of the 2007 subprime mortgage crisis any different from the machine that ground up the Polish immigrants who had come to Chicago pursuing their dream of a house, a comfortable life? Because of this novel, or rather because of its success, working conditions in the slaughterhouses were improved and workday hours reduced.

A few slaughterhouses remain in New York City's meatpacking district, but most have been replaced by restaurants and trendy cafés, fashion boutiques, and nightlife hotspots.

On the river that drains into the ocean, Pier 52 is visible across from the bold architecture of the Whitney Museum. No trace of its former structure can be seen. The pier has been widened and ships no longer dock at it. What good is knowing that there was once a thirteenth avenue, of which just a small section remains, that can only be seen from above on the High Line, because the Gansevoort Peninsula and its recreation areas were developed in a public-private partnership? Land won from the water and returned to it, diverted from its initial purpose. Time passes and destinations change. Culture spreads everywhere, just as the earth once intruded into shores and deltas. And yet, doesn't culture also find itself in a flood plain, like the land once claimed from and then returned to the water? Destined for submersion or erosion?

On this pier, Herman Melville performed his duties as a customs inspector for several years while writing the story of Billy Budd, inspired by an incident which involved one of his cousins. On the Internet, Benjamin Britten's opera has eclipsed the story of Billy Budd, no doubt because of some recent productions. In 2017, thanks to a new edition, the novella reemerged as the manuscript begun in 1888 and finished in 1891, or no, rather, completed and published by another hand in 1924 after it was found in a tin box by one of Melville's descendants. This sounds like one of those stories of discovered manuscripts from the late eighteenth or early nineteenth century that are meant to authenticate the tale that follows even though it sprang from the author's imagination exactly as its authentication had. What good is it to know, when on an evening walk along the High Line, that in an office below Melville was obliged to resume his administrative work once the success of *Moby Dick* had passed, although he never stopped writing, or that on Pier 52, where the light-colored sanitation-department building is located, or rather, adjacent to it, there was an enormous waste-incineration plant in which Wilhelm Reich's publications were burned in 1956? Six tons of paper, six tons of thoughts and ideas. Reich was sentenced to two years imprisonment for having discovered orgone—a source of energy both biological and cosmic—and publishing his discovery, and also for practicing medicine without a license. Did the censors take advantage of this charge to not only get rid of the inconvenient books of a writer who studied sexuality without the screen of morality but also those by a writer with nearly the same name, William Reich, a former member of the Communist Party in McCarthy-era America? Will anyone on the High Line, where the first lights are just going on in the apartments on the upper floors of the buildings that overlook it, think about Pier 52 below, on which Wilhelm Reich's books were burned for a second time—the first time was in 1935, in Nazi Germany, which Reich had fled initially to Austria, then to Scandinavian countries (Denmark, Sweden, Norway) and Great Britain, before crossing the Atlantic to the United States? Here too you hear other languages, but spoken by tourists or students from Europe or other countries in the Americas. On the High Line, you'd search in vain for illegal immigrants from Mexico, the Philippines, Central America—maybe they're hiding in the kitchens of the trendy bars and restaurants while the taxis driven by Pakistani immigrants glide through the twilight toward the airport . . .

I

Night. All lights are extinguished, even the moon has disappeared, and the rain is falling. But more than the rain, it's the darkness that floods everything. Darkness inundates the house, descends on it, streams in through the keyholes and cracks, pervades the building, swallowing up the flowers, erasing all shapes and contours in a space both full and fluid, something indistinct, primordial, from which life has perhaps retreated.

there was scarcely anything left of body or mind by which one could say, 'This is he' or 'This is she.'

Scarcely anything was left of the body or mind which would allow one to say, 'This is he' or 'This is she.' There was nothing left of the body or mind by which one could say, 'This is he' or 'This is she.' Nothing was left of a body or a mind by which one could be led to say, 'This is he' or 'This is she.'

Neither body nor mind, neither man nor woman: distinctions are erased in a uniform night. Is there anyone left? Any life? Is it before? Is it after? Does the world begin anew each night?

Especially on islands. *To the Lighthouse* is set on the Island of Skye. That's where Woolf has transposed her memories of childhood holidays in Cornwall. Certainly, Cornwall is a *land's end* and there are lighthouses offshore, in the open sea. But the lighthouse is on a small island, itself off a larger island, on which a family lives, finding refuge in a time called 'vacation', and this entire island archipelago lends the house, the sea, and the night a dimension of the absolute.

I'm circling. I'm here for something, or rather, against something. I filled out an application at the very last minute, as one does sometimes, not believing I had a chance, yet believing, grabbing the lifebuoy sent by fate, and soon after I received their answer. My proposal had been accepted, and the coherence I'd tried to give my idea—translating Virginia Woolf in Dresden, a text on time's destruction in a city once destroyed by war—had convinced them. Were there too few applicants? Had I really managed to connect two unrelated things? Translating a novel from English into French in German surroundings? It would be an experiment, I wrote. The striking strangeness of a language. Living on a kind of island so that I could immerse myself in the island created by the twenty-page section called "Time Passes" in the middle of Woolf's novel. You can justify anything if you make an effort. I didn't state the reason I was applying; it wasn't one you would express in an application. And even in Dresden, I dive into other words, which both take me farther away from and bring me closer to the heart of what I'm trying to avoid.

Ten years after Virginia Woolf's novel appeared, a film came out that was also set on an island, but one without a lighthouse at the time: *The Edge of the World*. A film by Michael Powell, shot on the island of Foula. In the movie, the island is called Hirta even though the map shown in close-up at the beginning corresponds to Foula's topography. In the movie, the island is in the Hebrides, although it was filmed in the Shetlands. A spatial transposition, just like in Virginia Woolf's novel. And yet, the story of *The Edge of the World*, about the inhabitants of an island who come to the conclusion that they can no longer live on it, is based on the actual story of Hirta, in the St Kilda archipelago, which was, in fact, evacuated over two days in late August 1930 on the request of the inhabitants—of whom there were only thirty-six left. Michael Powell was not given permission to film on the abandoned island and so he chose Foula, which was still inhabited, but whose nature, houses, and atmosphere seemed fitting. And it was almost as difficult to reach as Hirta.

Nothing stirred in the drawing-room or in the dining-room or on the staircase.

Nothing was stirring in the drawing room or in the dining room or on the staircase. Or on the stairs. In the parlor.

In the absence of movement, oddly, you hear the silence. You hold your breath. As if there were a moment of suspense. As if it were describing the scene of a crime and only the murderer and victim were missing.

To the Lighthouse does not have a narrator. It's the author who speaks and, one by one, examines each person—her characters. But in the second section of this three-part novel—how heavily these words, *section*, *novel*, *examine*, weigh compared to the work's airy grace, its oceanic fluidity—in the second section, "Time Passes" (although in the manuscript, the sections are not given titles), time does pass. There are no characters, or almost none. They appear at the beginning like shades, they come to open the door and put out the light; Mr. Carmichael resists a bit longer than the others, reading Virgil by candlelight, but he, too, finally extinguishes his light. Is he reading the *Aeneid* or the *Georgics*? Likely the *Georgics*, and perhaps this passage: "Or as the boundless ocean's God thou come, / Sole dread of seamen, till far Thule bow / Before thee," *tibi serviat ultima Thule,* Thule at the edge of the world. It's from this passage that Powell took the title of his film—*ultima Thule* and its English translation. Yes, Mr. Carmichael is no doubt reading one of the books of the *Georgics* and its evocation of the moment when day is as long as night, or its description of the winds and the rains, of sea birds flying swiftly, beating their wings, to the shelter of dry land.

—*To the Lighthouse* is published on May 5, 1927. On April 26, 1986, the Chernobyl nuclear accident occurs. Nothing seems to connect these two events—a book and the explosion of a nuclear reactor.

—In 1927 there are no nuclear power plants, and even though radium had been isolated for some time and its radioactivity known, the first power plants aren't built until the 1950s—first in the United States, then in the Soviet Union, then in France.

—How many of the people working in the Chernobyl nuclear power plant might have read *To the Lighthouse*? Can we confidently say none?

—The novel was translated in the Soviet Union in 1976 with the title *На маяк*, a literal transcription with the preposition indicating movement followed by the word for lighthouse—there is no article in Russian. It will be followed by *Mrs. Dalloway* in 1984, then *Flush* in 1986.

—What thoughts or ulterior motives, what coincidences led to this sequence?

—After these titles, readers would have to wait for the break up of the USSR, the collapse of the empire, for access to *The Waves, Orlando*, and *Between the Acts*.

—Chernobyl and the lighthouse—fifty-nine years apart.

—The test was done on the night of April 25–26, 1986. It was a safety test of the steam-turbine power system for the emergency feedwater pumps and its ability to keep the reactor running in the event of a loss of external power.

—At 1:23 a.m., local time, the test begins. The temperature in the vessel rises and it takes only forty seconds for the reactor to explode, or, more precisely, for a concrete slab to explode. A weight of 1,200 tons falls on the reactor and crushes it, and a fire spreads.

—A series of errors, negligence, and bad decisions compound the situation. The workers react late, they don't immediately understand—they don't want to know.

—The accident—it's initially called an accident or cloud—is first announced by Sweden, then confirmed by Russia in the evening.

—But the extent of the disaster, like that of all disasters, is measured only later.

Certain airs, detached from the body of the wind [. . .] *crept round corners and ventured indoors.*

Certains airs, détachés du corps du vent [. . .] rampaient autour des coins, s'aventuraient à l'intérieur. Certain airs, detached from the wind's body [. . .] slipped round corners and ventured indoors. Des souffles d'air, détachés du corps du vent, tournaient dans les recoins et s'aventuraient à l'intérieur. Drafts of air, detached from the body of the wind, rounded the corners and ventured indoors. Des souffles qui s'étaient détachés du vent, contournaient les angles, s'aventurant à l'intérieur. Certain airs that had detached themselves from the body of the wind crawled round corners, venturing indoors.

Nothing is satisfactory, in particular, how can *crept round corners* be rendered in French? Are these *corners* inside the house or outside, as the sentence's final word *indoors* seems to indicate? Thus the phrase follows the movement of the breeze, of the wind that blows outdoors while one of its tributaries—because the wind is like a river—rushes into the corners and flows through the house. S'engouffrait dans les recoins, pénétrait à l'intérieur. That's it, rushed into the corners, flowed indoors. The actions aren't successive but simultaneous. *Ventured indoors* extends, completes, explains *crept round corners.*

from the body of the wind (the house was ramshackle after all).

from the current of wind (the house, after all, was ramshackle). From the body of the wind (because the house was dilapidated).

Drafts of air enter through the rusted hinges, through the wood warped by the moist sea air. The wind, the breeze, the drafts bring movement into this apparently abandoned house—it is at the very least run down. Perhaps there are still occupants because occasionally there's the sound of a groan or the flash of a hand raised as if to clutch something, but this may be an illusion, a habit, the impossibility of imagining a house without occupants. In any case, the drafts of air seem to be the only life inside and they take things in hand, so to speak, *musingly*, asking questions of the flowers and those leavings that are the contents of the wastepaper basket, the torn letters, and the flowers, and the books . . . All are now open to the intruding airs, asking . . .

Were they allies? Were they enemies?

The war looms—without saying its name.

Thursday, May 5, 1927. "Book out. We have sold (I think) 1690 before publication—twice Dalloway. I write however in the shadow of the damp cloud of the Times Lit. Sup. review, which is an exact copy of the JsR. Mrs Dalloway review, gentlemanly, kindly, timid & praising beauty, doubting character, & leaving me moderately depressed. I am anxious about Time Passes. Think the whole thing may be pronounced soft, shallow, insipid, sentimental. [. . .] I know why I am depressed: a bad habit of making up the review I should like before reading the review I get."

Things improve over the following days. People start to react, to tell Virginia Woolf that it's her best book. Still, she suspects that no one has read it to the end; she notes that it's too soon, all while acknowledging that positive reviews have no effect whereas the negative reviews are almost stimulating. And then, ten days later—Monday, May 16—the book is "on its feet." A private concert of praise: Vanessa, Vita, Lady Ottoline Morrell, Clive Bell . . .

Two weeks later, in bed for a week with a severe headache. She resumes her diary on Monday, June 6, a Whit Monday. "I think, however, I am now almost an established figure—as a writer. They dont laugh at me any longer. Soon they will take me for granted. Possibly I shall be a celebrated writer. Anyhow, The Lighthouse is much more nearly a success, in the usual sense of the word, than any other book of mine."

Bodies pass on the streets, paying no attention to each other. Names are unsaid, but deep within each body slumbers something shared that is merely waiting to be awakened. One stranger passes another and a thought occurs to him, it catches him, and he doesn't know that the person he passed has had it, that this thought was passed from one to the other, that it will continue on its way to yet another, and so on, down the street, turning left, then reaching an intersection, multiplying in order to lodge in various minds and, little by little, not only to take root in their minds but also to express itself, to become word, to be exchanged, to spread and be accepted as self-evident, as a banality.

I'm elsewhere, in another city, another country. The language of my internal thoughts is not the one spoken here. Are we ultimately impenetrable? Will I never know the internal life playing out here? Will I pass like a silhouette, a shade, without knowing anyone?

On December 4, 1976, Benjamin Britten passed away in Aldeburgh, a small Suffolk town on the eastern coast of England. Aldeburgh still holds traces of a village called Slaughden that had been founded right on the coast. Several houses in the village were getting dangerously close to the water, or rather, the waters of the North Sea were advancing on them until these houses found themselves on the beach and finally, at the end of their run, were swallowed up by the waves during an unusually violent storm. Slaughden no longer exists, yet Aldeburgh retains its memory—the remains of a tower built early in the nineteenth century to fortify the coast and preserve it from a possible invasion by Napoleon's army. Britten's death was particularly devastating for a man more than two thousand kilometers away, across the sea, somewhere in Estonia. A composer. Arvo Pärt. The following year a work appeared: *Cantus in Memoriam Benjamin Britten.* Slightly more than seven and a half minutes of music and silence that opens with three peals of a bell, a death knell. The strings swell as the bell continues to toll, drowning under a wave of strings or emerging, alone. Both grief and the soothing possibility of consolation spread, even as the waves keep rolling, repetitively, staggered as in a canon, attempting, perhaps, to translate the monotony of loss that is tangible at every moment. Arvo Pärt has written that he had only just discovered Benjamin Britten's music and recognized its importance in itself and for him, its purity. In it, Pärt found a kinship and had hoped to meet Britten one day despite the distance and the political and administrative obstacles—the visas necessary to travel to the West—until the announcement of Britten's death suddenly put an end to that hope.

Depending on the concert, the cantus opens with a simple bell struck with a hammer or with chimes of metal tubes that dangle like the branches of a weeping willow or with chimes shaped like a xylophone hung from a tree. *Cantus*—the melody rises and falls like the consciousness of loss. One thinks of it, no longer thinks of it, or thinks of it with some solace, then thinks of it again with pain. Grief is not one endless plain; it is a series of hills and valleys, a rising and falling, the gradual acceptance of disaster. Absence settles in, it digs the way the sea sculpts the shore, continuously, stubbornly—and even if the water regularly withdraws, it always returns, relentlessly. Absence has the upper hand.

Tintinnabulation—this is Arvo Pärt's definition of one part of his music, adopting a word invented by Edgar Allan Poe in his poem *The Bells* to designate the persistent sound after the bell is rung. The earliest bells, it seems, were found in China and date from the third millennium BCE, perhaps earlier. Bells were also found in Egypt and Mesopotamia. They were used everywhere as a summons to gather. Were they utilitarian tools first or musical instruments? Both at once? It took some time for the Christian religion to adopt bells, since they were initially associated with pagan cults. Over the years, however, they ended up in towers, and from then on were inseparable from the architectural feature of churches called the bell tower. The bells called to prayer but also marked secular hours, signaling to the peasants when it was time to get up, to take a break from work, and to go to bed. They warned of storms—also hoping to stop them—and alerted of a shipwreck, a boat casting off, the arrival of an important person, or the arrival of a train. They accompanied the passage from life to death (there was a "passing bell" that signified someone was in their death throes) and funeral ceremonies, celebrated weddings, marked the opening of a judicial or parliamentary session or the beginning and end of a class. Each signal has a different form, sound, and purpose. Bells, Edgar Allan Poe's poem tells us, give a rhythm to the seasons of our lives, from the merry days of spring to the horror of the death knell. Today we hear them less often. We encounter them more frequently in tales of sunken cities (announcing the imminent catastrophe) than in daily life in cities or of an evening, in a concert.

But what after all is one night?

A night not in the sense of the opposite of day, but as a single night that can be counted. Only one. A night in the broad expanse of time. A minuscule point. There's that particular rhythm. *But what after all is one night?* Woolf could have written *but what is one night after all,* after all often being placed after the verb. But here, it's the rhythm that scans the phrase and decides the placement of the words. Rhythm is the essential element of writing, Woolf says somewhere. Night settles in. And in winter, it lasts. Night follows night. And in this world of bare trees that has followed autumn's splendor, you can hear the long sighing of a humanity that has not completely given up on the world.

The autumn trees, ravaged as they are, take on the flash of tattered flags kindling in the gloom of cool cathedral caves where gold letters on marble pages describe death in battle and how bones bleach and burn far away in Indian sands.

The autumn trees with ravaged limbs, utterly ravaged, in their ravage. Autumn trees, ravaged as they are, assume the flash of tattered flags blazing in the gloom of cool cathedral caves where gold letters on marble pages describe death in battle, recount death in combat. Where gold letters on marble pages describe death in battle and bones bleaching and burning far away in Indian sands. The autumn trees, for all their ravage, take on the flash of tattered flags glowing in the cool obscurity of the cathedral crypts where descriptions of death in battle and how bones bleach and burn far away in Indian sands are inscribed in gold letters on marble pages.

In the desolate winter or autumn landscape—there is no spring or summer—the only human presence is that of the war. Human beings are there to die, not to live. What lives is the earth and especially the sea. Humans haven't really disappeared, that's not the case, or at least not yet. However, they are no longer the phrase's essential subject, but its object. They are not in the nominative case but in the accusative. The trees—subject—take on the flash of flags—direct object and a trace of human presence. The war—*the nights are now full of wind and destruction*—is present everywhere without speaking its name. Of course, the waves crash onto the shore but their movement, violent as it is, doesn't destroy anything or doesn't yet destroy. It's the course of things. They advance and withdraw. But if someone wakes in the night because of the noise, the thundering, and gets up to walk along the beach as before, in peace time—during the day or in the evening—looking for an answer to existential questions, he won't find it. Because it's night? Because it's war? Because it never can be found?

Arvo Pärt is not the first to have introduced bells into a piece of music. In the fifth movement of the *Symphonie fantastique*, the "Songe d'une nuit de Sabbat," dream of a witches' sabbath, just before the third minute, Berlioz brings in their characteristic tolling. The movement begins softly but something is brewing, and the kettledrums underscore the disquiet to which the woodwinds' lightness paradoxically contributes—through sudden changes of rhythm. Then the bell sets in: a few isolated tolls and its dialogue with the horn. An annunciation of fate. The bell is too high to sound a death knell, and yet it portends strange events before falling silent and letting the sabbath night unfold.

To the Lighthouse—Mrs. Ramsay's death is announced in brackets. The characters no longer have the upper hand in the novel. They will regain it in the third section, "The Lighthouse." It's the elements that act, especially the sea and the wind; it's the house that takes center stage, and the best proof for this are the few lines that close the brief third chapter of "Time Passes," about the passage of time, if one can call this vignette, this poem in prose, a chapter.

[*Mr. Ramsay, stumbling along a passage stretched his arms out one dark morning but Mrs. Ramsay having died rather suddenly the night before he stretched his arms out. They remained empty.*]

How to translate this? The syntax is confusing. [Mr. Ramsay, trébuchant dans un couloir, étendit les bras par un sombre matin, mais, Mrs. Ramsay étant morte assez soudainement la nuit précédente, il étendit les bras. Ils restèrent vides.] He stretched his arms out, but he stretched his arms out. Ils restèrent vides. Qui restèrent vides. Qui demeurèrent vides. Mr. Ramsay, trébuchant dans le couloir, tendit les bras par un noir matin, mais Mrs. Ramsay étant morte plutôt soudainement la nuit précédente, il étendit les bras. Qui demeurèrent vides. Why is there no past participle for the French verb *mourir*? Why do we have to resort to the verb *décéder*? Mrs. Ramsay ayant décédé la nuit précédente. Étant décédée dans la nuit. In French, it sounds like a death announcement, whereas the English original sounds much more natural. Getting back to étant morte . . . In any case, the problem remains—the *but*. He *stretched his arms out . . . but . . . he stretched his arms out.* And then the period after *out*; the sentence stops and leaves the conjunction incomplete. Is it a typographical error that is reproduced in different versions from the first edition? Sustained carelessness? A decision to introduce a rupture? A punctuation error with a period instead of the expected comma? *but Mrs. Ramsay having died rather suddenly the night before, he stretched his arms out, they remained empty.* You're even tempted to add *and they remained empty*. But there is no "and" and there is a period.

The puzzle is contained in the brackets, which seems to indicate that Mrs. Ramsay's death, even though she is the central character at the heart of the novel, is a chance event like so many others, an incident on the way to the lighthouse (because the title, fundamentally, indicates an itinerary, both physical and spiritual, leading to the lighthouse). And yet, because of the odd syntax, the bracketed lines give us pause or, rather, make us stumble like Mr. Ramsay over this death. The commas after *but* and *before* were added after the first edition. Why, since they don't change much and interrupt the rhythm of the sentence? The 1930 American edition—the first British edition is dated 1927—differs slightly and presents this passage in a more immediately comprehensible version. *Mr. Ramsay, stumbling along a passage one dark morning, stretched his arms out, but Mrs. Ramsay having died rather suddenly the night before, his arms, though stretched out, remained empty.* Here, we no longer stumble. The sentence flows smoothly and reaches its end without impediment.

Is this really what Virginia Woolf wanted? She who returned to this section constantly? April 18, 1926—a Sunday: "Yesterday I finished the first part of To the Lighthouse, &

today began the second. I cannot make it out—here is the most difficult abstract piece of writing—I have to give an empty house, no people's characters, the passage of time, all eyeless & featureless with nothing to cling to: well, I rush at it, & at once scatter out two pages. Is it nonsense, is it brilliance? Why am I so flown with words, & apparently free to do exactly what I like? When I read a bit it seems spirited too; needs compressing, but not much else." And then on Tuesday, May 25: "I have finished—sketchily I admit—the 2nd part of To the Lighthouse—& may, then, have it all written over by the end of July." *Sketchily*. A draft. In the very first version, the handwritten one, there are no brackets, and we don't learn of Mrs. Ramsay's death until Mrs. McNab arrives to do the cleaning and to assume all human presence in the house. "I love / To walk the heights, from whence no earlier track / Slopes gently downward to Castalia's spring," Virgil writes in Book III of the *Georgics*, perhaps the very one that Mr. Carmichael is reading.

To go where no one has yet gone, exploring, discovering. I'd have liked to be able write and follow unmarked paths, then work and rework them to turn them into a landscape. But I've never known how, I've never tried, I took up other things, the transfer, the transcription, the attempt to restore a written text as closely as possible in a different language. And this is what I'm trying to do, here in Dresden.

On a stone obelisk in the middle of a broad, central avenue, there are several black plaques. The bottom one explains the monument's intention in white capital letters. Dedicated to unknown stars that have disappeared in explosions that dispersed the atomic nuclei of which we are constituted into interstellar space. In fourteen lines. Right and left margins justified. The size of the letters varies—or rather, four lines are written in smaller letters to fit the words into the same length. EXPLOSIONS / DISPERSED INTO / INTERSTELLAR SPACE. Maybe it's just an impression. The letters may be the same size and it's the spacing between each line that is tighter. On the opposite side of the obelisk, there are six plaques, also black with inscriptions in white, capital letters. In memory of SN 1006, a supernova observed on April 17, 1006 in the constellation Centaurus. In memory of SN 1054, a supernova observed on July 4, 1054 in the constellation Taurus. The supernovas are numbered according to the year in which they were observed, were discovered. The list continues. In memory of SN 1181, a supernova observed on August 6, 1181 in the constellation Cassiopeia. In memory of SN 1572, a supernova observed on November 11, 1572 in the constellation Cassiopeia. In memory of SN 1604, a supernova observed on October 9, 1604 in the constellation Ophiuchus. In memory of SN 1987, a supernova in the Large Magellanic Cloud observed on February 23, 1987. According to Wikipedia, a supernova is the luminous explosion of a star during its last evolutionary stages. So isn't the date indicated not actually that of the star's death but instead that of its discovery? In a cemetery, how could it be any different? This is confirmed by the bottom plaque on the base of the obelisk dedicated to stars that have disappeared. Dedicated to the unknown stars that have disappeared. On another side, there are two more plaques. C215. And the image of an explosion. C215 is the artist's name—graffiti artists' names are often letters followed by numbers. C215. SP 38. What do these letters mean, and what do the numbers indicate? C as in city, C as in celestial? Is it a protest, a way to differentiate street art from traditional art signed with the artist's first and last names? When we come upon the obelisk monument to stars that have disappeared, we don't ask ourselves that question. Instead, we let the poetry of these vanishings enter us and suddenly the loss we have come to mourn takes on cosmic dimensions and that is some help.

I have come to mourn someone.

To decenter—everything shows that you must center and decenter at the same time. Change your perspective. That's what Virginia Woolf does in "Time Passes." The perspective is changed, decentered; it switches from the characters who inhabit the novel to the space that contains them. The house. What do those we love do when we don't see them? How do they walk along the street? What is he thinking of? And she? They? I will never penetrate the intimate thoughts of the person facing me. I'll never know if what he or she says corresponds exactly to what they are thinking. The *suspension of disbelief* that Coleridge called for doesn't apply exclusively to reading. But also to life. Suspend mistrust. Believe what people tell you. What happens to those we no longer see?

So with the house empty and the doors locked and the mattresses rolled round . . . signs of the withdrawal of people, of the characters, of human life . . .

Far away, in a distant land, outside a city named Pripyat and a power plant called Chernobyl, covering an area of roughly thirty square kilometers, there is an exclusion zone, also called the forbidden zone, from which 135,000 people were evacuated. It has been completely devoid of human presence for more than thirty years, just as the house in *To the Lighthouse* was uninhabited for ten years. There are spots on the map, and this is called leopard-spot contamination. But designating the exclusion zone does not allow for a complicated pattern, so a circle with a radius of thirty kilometers is drawn around the power plant, an enormous territory—the area of Luxembourg—in which it is forbidden to live. In order to be certain, the houses in the abandoned villages are destroyed. Abnormalities appear on the animals. Over a few weeks, the pine trees turn red and die. The forest becomes known as the Red Forest, one of the new names created by Chernobyl. Cities die, cities are born or reborn—this is what the century has taught us. We believed—we, the human race—believed that we inhabited the earth, that we owned, ruled, controlled it—all these words sound outdated. We are merely temporary residents.

At the entrance to the zone there is a barrier, a customs post where entrants are screened and their authorization and reason for being there is checked. Most are scientists, but for some time now, buses of tourists have been coming for periods that are limited enough, they're assured, to avoid any negative effects from the radiation. Movies are also filmed there, documentaries too. Occasionally, feature films. Science fiction. Television movies. And recently, a television series. Meanwhile in Kyiv, one of the first institutions founded in newly independent Ukraine was the museum of Chernobyl. The residents of Pripyat, where the power-plant workers lived, were essentially evacuated to the capital, a hundred and ten kilometers away.

In the museum, where everything is identified and explained, there is a model of the reactor and the white uniforms of the liquidators. There are also photographs of evacuated children and the identity papers of those who died battling the fire, believing they were simply putting out a blaze when they were fighting against invisible particles that would spread all over Europe, fighting a new kind of war in which the enemy had taken on the deceptive appearance of fire. In the last room, dedicated to the spread of the "accident," the cloud's trajectory is displayed. And yet some people, a guide says, still believe that the cloud spared their country.

Losing someone—the silence that opens a piece of music. It's the background on which our lives are drawn; it's what gives them form. I can't say that I see her face, although now and then it becomes vaguely recognizable—besides, I've never known what a mental image is. But I do hear her voice, strangely, without words, wordless music—or the memory of words heard, the shadow of words said. Like the traces of human life in the house of "Time Passes."

What people had shed and left [. . .] *those alone kept the human shape and in the emptiness indicated how once they were filled and animated.*

Les choses qui avaient été remisées, the things that had been shed, no, not the passive voice, the *people* must be present because it's precisely a question of their absence. Les choses que les gens avaient remisées, laissées, elles seules gardaient la forme humaine, elles seules gardaient une forme humaine, ou forme humaine, et par leur vide indiquaient qu'elles avaient été autrefois pleines et animées. . . . and with their emptiness indicated that they used to be filled and animated. Ou qu'elles furent autrefois pleines et animées. Or that they had once been Ou qu'elles étaient. Or that they once were. *La concordance des temps*, the sequence of tenses. No two languages have the same system and often the choice of tense is crucial . . . Shoes, a hunting cap, coats and skirts in the wardrobe. Clothes become useless; their limp forms keeping the human shapes of those who had once filled them. The people are now nothing more than a memory contained in the objects they'd used. Humankind. This novel covers this subject in its own fashion well before Robert Antelme wrote about it in his book, *L'espèce humaine*. Through the precariousness of individual fates, Virginia Woolf presents (in the primary sense of shows) the fate of the entire species; the common fate of all human beings, our fate. But we are not alone. Our lives are connected, bound to other elements. The lighthouse. The sea. And inside the house,

how once the looking glass had held a face;

The face is not reflected in the mirror; it's the mirror that holds the face. How the looking-glass once held a face. A face, a voice. Yes, I hear her voice, but the words she's saying don't reach me.

—And yet people live here, having returned several days after the evacuation. Old women, mostly—babushkas, as they're called. Are they actually grandmothers? There are few men, that's true. The women tend their gardens and they are allowed to do so.

—Where do you want us to go? they ask. We've always lived here. Risks from radioactivity? We'll bear them, just as we do our rheumatism. They're no more visible, no more real than rheumatism, less, in fact. And so far, painless.

—The names of the vanished cities vary with the eras, swallowed up by water or ghost towns left behind from the Gold Rush. Aztec cities destroyed by unknown cataclysms—war, famine, there are many possible explanations. Cities buried in earthquakes.

—Some are rebuilt, while others sink into oblivion. Of the latter, a few have traversed the ages with their names and legends . . . Atlantis . . . Vineta . . .

Foula—at the edge of the world, or rather Hirta. An island on which a sailboat is landing. What a fragile thing it is next to the cliffs facing it, but the boat docks with three passengers on board, two men, one woman. The man in the black cap is at the center of the story. The island is deserted, dotted with stone houses. Their windows are barred, their roofs timbers are exposed. On a wall hangs a post-office sign with some of the letters partly erased. The island is deserted, the house abandoned, and the screen white. This is what I'm seeking. Everything that shows signs of absence. In this section of *To the Lighthouse,* many words express this void: *emptiness, a world hollowed out,* and *shadow, reflect*, along with the ghostly presence of shadows, of reflections, even the silhouettes, the contours, the forms, and the echo. Each thing hides another, every appearance conceals not its own reality but another reality.

I left some time ago. To go there. To come here. To Dresden. Not to a deserted island, but to a formerly destroyed city. Destroyed long ago—not that long. Seventy-five years, it's a lot, it's not a lot, it's real, it's unreal. But the city is there and has the same name and endeavors to conserve the memory of a night of aerial bombardment by inscribing it on commemorative plaques mounted on restored monuments and through celebrations. At the same time, it attempts to erase the memory of the bombing with historically accurate reconstructions of the buildings that were its glory. Cities are bodies with slowly forming scars, and they are rejuvenated all the more effectively when they have a river flowing through their centers, marking two shores that make one think of reconciliation—because bridges are the first things to be rebuilt.

There I was, in that city, walking along the empty streets. It was mid-autumn, November, that winterlike month. The early evening seemed later than midnight and, as if to reinforce this impression, there was not a soul to be seen, not even on the streets of the city center, the rebuilt old city. The emptiness made the tall silhouettes of the unrestored churches seem menacing—as if the city were not inhabited by people but by enormous stone guards ready to defend it at any cost. Occasionally, my steps echoed, making me feel almost afraid. What had happened in these streets? It was as if the city itself had taken over and eliminated all the residents. I'd rented a room near the Elbe. When I looked out the rather high window, I could see a slice of the river. But mostly I saw the mass of the gingko tree's golden foliage, which did justice to its nickname of "the forty-crown tree." Many more than forty, each golden fan gleamed in the morning sun. I had the opportunity to stay several weeks, and I was already wondering if I should prolong my stay past the stipend's allotted time. Nothing was calling me back, the room here was available—there were few tourists this time of year—it was affordable, and, with my computer, I could work as well here as anywhere.

The freedom to stay any place whatsoever for an extended time is one of the advantages of an untethered life. I obeyed the laws of chance, followed impulses and, because life had ensured—or had I?—that I would follow its paths alone and only occasionally meet someone who would briefly become a companion, I enjoyed the advantages. Facing the tower of black stone at night, which seemed to be coming toward me since its mass was so sharply distinguished from the other buildings—there are, after all, several depths of black—I expected someone to appear. Someone I knew or didn't know. I thought of . . . how can I put it, what should I call it? It wasn't a ghost or a shadow—these words or things were still too substantial—it was a parallel life that I was leading, as if moments from the past were there, on another path, as if I only had to turn my eyes to see them and, above all, to feel them. But that still wasn't it. These days, people would laugh if I said the word and I, myself, hardly dared speak it. And yet, in the shadow of the black tower of the Church of the Holy Cross—it too destroyed in wars, fires, bombardments, and rebuilt each time, spanning the arc of religious architecture, from Gothic to Baroque, from Baroque to Classicism, then to Art Nouveau—in the shadow of its tower, the word came naturally to me, imposed itself on me: the soul. This is what was accompanying me, the soul of a life that was no more and nonetheless still was; something that lingered, that remained, that was settling within me or, rather, something that was inside me which I was discovering, someone's life, moments that certainly weren't mine but that I had shared, scenes, images, visions—and the sound of a voice.

—The Coventry Blitz, everyone knows of it without necessarily knowing the date. It was on the November 14, 1940 that the Luftwaffe attacked in the cynically code-named Operation Moonlight Sonata. Only ruins were left of the church and the city. The bombing caused nearly six hundred deaths.

—On Friday, November 15, 1940, Virginia Woolf writes in her diary, *Coventry almost destroyed.*

—All that remains of the cathedral is the bell-tower, a wall, and the frames of several windows, through which daylight falls—the sky.

—Two charred beams were found, one lying on top of the other in the shape of a cross, by chance. They were bound together. Nails from the roof timbers were also assembled to form a cross. A new altar was soon built, under the open sky, and in the back of the chancel, two words were engraved—*Father Forgive*—a plea for forgiveness.

—The two crosses, the one of charred beams, *Charred Cross*, and the one made of nails, *Cross of Nails*, have become symbols of peace and reconciliation.

—Crosses were made from nails found in the ruins. And when there were no longer enough nails to fill the orders, more were brought in from a German prison.

—There now are many of these crosses in German churches—in the Church of the Holy Cross in Dresden, for example.

—In 1962, the new cathedral was consecrated near the preserved ruins of the old one. For the occasion, Benjamin Britten's *War Requiem* was played the first time, in May, with three soloists, Dietrich Fischer-Dieskau, Galina Vichnevskaïa, and Peter Pears. A German, a Russian, and an Englishman—from the nations previously at war.

—Mingled with the Latin are verses of Wilfred Owen, killed in the previous war, the First.

—The *War Requiem* was also played in Dresden, in 1965, on the twentieth anniversary of the bombing, and then again, in 2008, in the Frauenkirche, the Church of Our Lady, destroyed by British bombs to avenge Coventry, it was said, and left in ruins by the East German regime. It was rebuilt after the fall of the Wall and reconsecrated sixty years after its destruction.

—And so closes the tragic but hope-filled circle from destruction to reconciliation.

That evening, on the streets of Dresden, passing the tower of the large Church of the Holy Cross, I had a different requiem in mind. Not its melody—it's difficult to speak of melody—but the circumstances of its creation. The composer's name was Heinrich Johannes Wallmann. I'd just discovered him by chance in my random research into Dresden, because this city, which I'd disliked at first, now fascinated me. I'd disliked it because it was too focused on itself, too hostile to strangers—the strong presence of extremist and xenophobic movements was often attributed to the fact that this city happened to be in a kind of "Valley of the Clueless," in a region where, at the time of the Iron Curtain, there was no reception of West German radio broadcasts. In other words, Dresden residents were said to have blindly believed the regime's truths because, unlike the rest of the GDR, they had no way of enjoying the antidote of the West. It is true that Dresden is near the Czech border and is not far from Poland, both countries of the so-called East. The closest Western region was Bavaria, and reaching it required crossing forests and mountains that even radio waves seemed to find impassible. Still, aside from the fact that this explanation credits West German television with many pedagogical and democratic virtues, it falls rather short.

Wallmann. On the fiftieth anniversary of the bombing of Dresden, November 12, 1995, beginning at exactly 9:30 p.m. and lasting until 10:12 p.m., the bells of Dresden rang. 129 bells in 47 churches. Each tone had been individually studied and recorded. There was no rehearsal, not even a partial one. Everything was meant to happen live, in the moment—and to happen only once. The score had no notes, just indications of the place and the moment when each particular bell was to toll. Assistants wearing headphones waited in the churches, near the bells, for the signal that would set off the bells, now instruments in an orchestra that would exist only one night between 9:30 and 10:12. A little like the *Symphony of Factory Sirens*, created by Arseny Avraamov in Baku in 1922 using factory sirens, foghorns, the Soviet flotilla in the Caspian Sea, hydro-airplanes, cannons, locomotives, and choirs. Everything performed live and in public and conducted by Avraamov, for that moment the leader of an incredible orchestra that included the entirety of the port. There were bells in his symphony too, about six minutes in, tolling all out, until their ringing was progressively swallowed up by the sound of a circling airplane. Wallmann had composed several dozen minutes only for bells, which we can still hear because they were broadcast on the radio—on Deutschlandradiokultur, MDR Kultur, BBC London, and Radio Washington DC—and are accessible on the Internet. The residents of Dresden had gathered that night in the city squares or near the Elbe, or on the hills above the river for better acoustics. Depending on their position, each auditor had a different perception of the work, and as a result, the radio broadcast, later distributed on a CD, offers only a partial experience. You would have had to be everywhere at once or to stand in different spots, one after the other, or simultaneously at all the compass points because the bells were activated according to their location. But perhaps Wallmann had wanted each listener to be an element of an abstract ideal audience covering the entire expanse of the musical work.

In my research, I'd read that the Dresden churches had refused to allow their bells to make profane sounds and have them reduced to musical instruments. And yet, there had been far worse uses. During the wars—in particular the two world wars—the bells had been requisitioned, just as men had, for the army.

Having passed the Church of the Holy Cross's imposing tower, I continued along an equally deserted street—turning around occasionally because I had the feeling someone was silently following me—and I had a quasi-vision of a mass of people in movement, dozens or hundreds of people in war-torn countries who were charged with taking down the bells. They couldn't be thrown from the bell-towers and broken. They were divided into categories according to an established classification: bells of artistic value, which had to be preserved unconditionally; bells of some value, which were reserved in case of emergency; and bells that were to be melted down. In Germany, this initiative expanded, and some sources report 44 per cent of the bells were melted down in the First World War and 77 per cent in the Second. Bells were requisitioned in the occupied countries as well. Fewer in France, it was said, because the Vichy government wanted to preserve good relations with the Church and favored melting bronze statues of figures in the republic rather than Joan of Arc or the Virgin Mary.

The nocturnal streets became superimposed with black-and-white photographs I'd seen on the Internet of bells waiting to be transported to places called bell cemeteries, or *Glockenfriedhöfe*. I even found a reproduction of a newspaper article from the end of the First World War, illustrated with a photograph found on a German prisoner of war of a train loaded with bells destined for Germany and its war effort. Just like in 1870, the article said and concluded: "The Germans have certainly remained what they were forty-eight years ago: thieves and villains." I imagined the silence of the villages deprived of their bells, where the hours passed unmarked. A kind of diurnal night. A time that passed differently. But I walked and walked, returning to my sparse room, furnished with only the essentials: a bed, a wardrobe, a writing desk, and a rather high window looking onto the gold of a ginkgo tree.

INTERLUDE

The disused rail tracks are now given over to vegetation, planted with birches, gray birches that are lit by discreet spotlights hidden in the ground, lending the urban landscape silvery reflections in the evening. What trains once ran along these tracks, what axles rolled over the few kilometers of the High Line? The rail network had been laid to service the slaughterhouses, warehouses, and factories, and to transport merchandise that arrived at the Hudson River port. Initially, the tracks were at street level and an entire neighborhood sprang up around this new mode of transport. But people weren't used to trains, and kept walking or driving their horse-drawn vehicles as if nothing had changed, unaware of the danger. To avoid the accidents, men on horseback were hired as, in a sense, crossing guards without crossings to warn of oncoming trains. The guard rode ahead of the train, waving a red flag during the day, a red lantern at night. Because this was not enough to prevent accidents, the city decided to elevate the rail line. The elevated rails connected to the warehouses' upper floors, so trains could be unloaded directly into the buildings. This was how the High Line began its noisy, animated life in 1934, which lasted until 1980. Night and day, its din joined the traffic on the avenues, and at the end of the line, enormous elevators stood ready to carry the merchandise into the city below, where trucks waited to be filled before setting off down the night streets to make deliveries to other neighborhoods in New York or to other cities . . .

For a long time now, architects have sought to expand cities vertically to compensate for the limits to horizontal expansion. They still do. The High Line sometimes recalls Hugh Ferris's drawings, inspired by the projects of Harvey Wiley Corbett, who imagined multi-level elevated tracks—pedestrians on broad galleries running along buildings with "ground floors" that were raised well above street level, which was given over to cars and public-transportation traffic. Imagine, as you look down on traffic, what a city conceived on the High Line model would be like with features that architects now recommend: towers planted with greenery, residential units on bridges—slender forms in black and white rising toward the sky, which served and still serve as inspiration for science-fiction films.

Delicate flowers have overgrown the rails. Asters of all varieties and colors, twisted leaf garlic, red clover, wild basil—the yellow and mauve are joined with a green so pale it almost seems white, and form a flowery mosaic of which the toiling city below is oblivious. Grasses and wild plants vary with the seasons. The forms, scents, and colors change. *Panicum virgatum*, switchgrass, a bunchgrass that comes from the prairies of the midwestern United States and adorns itself with a red spikelets in spring and pink flowers in summer. In winter, it is dormant. It's also called wild redtop. It came from the prairies, where it was considered a weed. But the High Line granted it asylum, despite its bad reputation, knowing that this grass offers animals shelter from the cold and can also be used as a biofuel.

Is it H. G. Wells's novel *The First Men in the Moon* that has one society of horribly exploited slaves underground and another above ground that can breathe and move freely in the open air?

Here, on the High Line, you feel revived, only what you can see exists, your senses are alert, everything has value, significance, a certain vividness, life is in color. On the High Line, people know how to avoid bumping into each other, everyone walks at their own pace without hindering others, and hope rises as the lights go on.

11

—You could say that the great concern of the twentieth century was the unconscious, its emergence—its revelation, its examination. That many inhabitants of the twentieth century were adventurers of the unconscious.

—Let's say, then, that the great concern of the twenty-first century will be consciousness, not its discovery, but its exploration, its definition and its limits.

—Do animals have a consciousness? Do trees? And robots? Does artificial intelligence—to what extent?

—An anthropology of algorithms has just been created—a conjunction of contradictory concepts—in order to study them and measure their margin of autonomy, their decision-making ability. In other words, to know if they have some form of consciousness.

those stray airs, advance guards of great armies, blustered in, brushed bare boards, nibbled and fanned, met nothing in bedroom or drawing-room that wholly resisted them but only hangings that flapped, wood that creaked, the bare legs of tables, saucepans and china already furred, tarnished, cracked.

ces airs vagabonds, no, no demonstrative pronoun—often you have to adapt and translate an indefinite article with a definite one or the other way around, you have to make mysterious adjustments—les airs vagabonds, gardes avancés des grandes armées, ou avant-garde de grandes armées, tempêtaient, ou entraient en tempêtant, effleuraient les planches nues, les parquets nus, les sols nus, stray airs, advance guards of great armies or avant-garde of great armies, stormed in or blew in stormily, brushed bare the bare boards, the bare parquet floors, the bare floors—but with floors alone the vision of wood is lost—mordillaient, attisaient, ne rencontraient rien dans la chambre ou au salon qui leur résistât pleinement mais seulement des rideaux, des tentures qui claquaient, du bois qui craquait, les pieds nus des tables, des casseroles et de la porcelaine déjà entartrées, ternies, craquelées.

What a muddle. For one thing, those wandering drafts of air in the house that should encounter solid objects—human presence consists of resistance—instead meet only their own substance, malleable, airy, supple, shifting. Virginia Woolf's style, so difficult to translate, is marked by juxtapositions, by successive flights and soft landings when the sentences aren't left in a state of suspension.

Les courants d'air vagabonds, à l'avant-garde des grandes armées, pénétraient en tempête, effleuraient le sol nu, rongeaient, rafraîchissaient, ne se heurtaient, dans la chambre, au salon, à aucune résistance mais seulement au battement des rideaux, au craquement du bois, aux pieds dénudés des tables, au tartre, au ternissement et au craquèlement des casseroles et de la porcelaine. The stray airs, advance guards of great armies, stormed in, brushing the bare floor, nibbled, were refreshed, met no resistance in bedroom or drawing room except for curtains that flapped, boards that creaked, bare table legs, scaling, tarnish, and cracks on the saucepans and china.

Does a translation convince when verbs are replaced with nouns? Doesn't that weigh down the sentences a little, a lot? And then *fanned*, the image of a fan, so light, rendered with *rafraîchir*, refresh, which is too long, but *fraîchir*, freshened, wouldn't work either. English-French dictionaries give *attiser*, to fan the flames, but that is exactly the opposite—there's no fire here, just air, and what is more immaterial, more difficult to grasp than currents of air? Besides, shouldn't it be currents of air rather than stray airs? Of breaths of air? The house's inhabitants are gone and the air takes possession of it, just as earlier the mirrors took the initiative of knowing what they were reflecting.

There was a mirror in the small bathroom next to the room I was renting with a shower, a sink, and this mirror above it. It wasn't big enough to see anything but my face. As if the rest of my body no longer existed. Should I continue regardless or try to find a version of each sentence that is more or less satisfactory? *Advance guards of great armies* is an echo of war, again, the Great War. The war intrudes in furtive echoes throughout the prose poem that is "Time Passes," as does all activity, all human presence. The tonalities are reversed. A major key for objects, for what we call nature, a minor key for humans. A new path for literature. A new way of understanding the world.

Now, day after day, light turned, like a flower reflected in water, its clear image on the wall opposite.

Maintenant, jour après jour, la lumière tournait, comme une fleur reflétée dans l'eau, son image claire sur le mur opposé. What can we understand by this literal translation? First of all, is *turned* used intransitively or is it separated from its object, *its clear image*, by the metaphor of the flower's reflection in water? That would give: Now, day after day, light, like a flower reflected in water, turned its clear image on the wall opposite, that is, on the wall opposite the mirror. But what does "turned its image" mean? Probably that shapes projected onto the wall by the light shift over the course of the days, and that they flow like water, they follow the sun's position in the sky. What time of year is it? We don't know. We merely follow the movement of light over the facing wall. Et jour après jour la lumière se mouvait, comme le reflet d'une fleur dans l'eau, projetant une image de clarté sur le mur opposé. And day after day, the light moved like the reflection of a flower in water projecting its clear image on the wall opposite. "Projecting" is an addition. But is it possible to adopt the point of view that, even though it lengthens the sentence, this word helps clarify it? And that projection is already implicit, in a way, in the image of the image? Also, in the typescript, *clear image* was *sharp image*, and was kept that way in the first American edition. But the English edition had *clear*, and it's the original edition. Sharp, *aiguisée*, clear, *claire*: maybe I should use *vive*, vivid, which is between the two, since it's light that is being qualified, the distinctness of the image it is projecting. *Nette*, lucid, could be a solution.

"Time Passes," *To the Lighthouse*, the book is as much about light as it is about time. And what a beautiful word, *lighthouse*; the French word *phare* is also beautiful, but we don't hear the light even if we imagine the beam. The German word, *Leuchtturm*, the illuminating tower, is closer even if the light of *Leucht* has a weaker connection to the blazing sonority of *light* than the more commonly used *Licht*, and it doesn't offer as *sharp* and *clear* an image.

The bears have come back, or rather, they've come, since they'd never lived in this part of Ukraine or anywhere in Ukraine, and the Przewalski's horses have been released into the exclusion zone. In a documentary entitled *Chernobyl: A Natural History?*, we are told that the oldest horses and sick ones were chosen for the experiment, so as not to put the future of this endangered species at risk. But contrary to all expectations, the Przewalski's horses thrived and multiplied so successfully that their numbers doubled from two dozen in 1998 to nearly fifty after two decades. It's a mystery, the scientists say. The animals in the exclusion zone have very high levels of radioactivity, but they live normally and seem in perfect health.

As for the flora it, too is thriving. In the Red Forest, the withered pines have given way to birch trees. Where there once were fields of wheat—didn't we learn that Ukraine was once the Soviet Union's breadbasket—there are now trees and grasses and, once again, streams. A kind of reincarnation. In memory of a previous life. What human work destroyed is restored by its disappearance. Both the same and different. This is another thing that scientists are trying to understand. They have set up laboratories in the heart of the exclusion zone. Every day they cross the borders and return to the edge of the zone in the evening. Some even live there. A laboratory is squatting in a former nursery school. The director planted a vegetable garden. He runs experiments, collects data. The cherries are radioactive, but the radioactivity is concentrated in the pit, so you can eat the fruit flesh. Potatoes and cucumbers are not a problem. But grapes, black currants, and sorrel are out of the question—their levels are dangerous. The scientists spend their days measuring.

The sievert is their preferred unit of measurement. Named after a Swedish scientist, this unit indicates the health risk of ionizing radiation on human beings. The average dose is 4mSv. Levels up to 20m are considered very low; 20m to 200m is low; 200m to 2,000m is medium—in other words, up to 2 sieverts. Levels between 2 and 10 are strong and over 10, very strong. Levels of 5 and above are, in principle, lethal. The average dose to Chernobyl liquidators was 100mSv, a dose considered weak but which, nonetheless, had devastating effects. And the firefighters received doses of 250mSv. Survivors of Hiroshima had been exposed to doses up to 500mSv. But the amounts vary depending on the sites—not contaminated sites, but websites. Still, they all agree on 5 as the lethal dose. Researchers in the exclusion zone measure the radiation levels of everything there—animals, trees, insects, plants, ground, underground, flowers, even the rusted combine-harvester left behind. They roam the forests with red, orange, or yellow dosimeters in hand. These look like remote controls, but the shows they turn on are strange. Why have such elevated levels of radiation, even if much lower than in the first weeks after the disaster, not destroyed or damaged all life in the zone? This is one of the questions the scientists are trying to answer.

So loveliness reigned and stillness, and together made the shape of loveliness itself, a form from which life had parted;

The English love semicolons, and Virginia Woolf loved them even more. They give her novels a rhythm, with brief pauses that encourage the flow. Touch and go. It starts with the first, with the second word in the sentence. *Loveliness.* What does it mean and how do I translate it? Is it merely beauty? Charm? Et reignait le charme, le calme (to keep the effect of rhyme), et ils faisaient ensemble la forme du charme même (*faire* doesn't work for "made"), une forme d'où la vie s'était absentée.

Et régnait le charme, le calme, ils façonnaient ensemble la forme de la beauté, forme d'où la vie s'était absentée. It's not bad as far as sound goes, even if some aspects are sacrificed. The repetition of *loveliness*, for example—but repetition is awkward in French, they say, and *itself* has disappeared—and so many things disappear in this story . . .

solitary like a pool at evening, far distant, seen from a train window, vanishing so quickly that the pool, pale in the evening, is scarcely robbed of its solitude, though once seen.

The beauty, the poetry. Every attempt at translation is bound to fail. Let's give it a try—with a sigh, but without getting discouraged. Solitaire comme un étang le soir, au loin, vu depuis la fenêtre d'un train, disparaissant si vite que cet étang, pâle dans le soir, est à peine ravi à sa solitude, bien que vu. Would *bien qu'ayant été vu*, despite having been seen, be more correct in French than *bien que vu*, though seen? But is translation about being more correct? *Though once seen.* It's a light touch, direct and plain, simple. Simplest is best. But is it really necessary to use *étang* for *the pool*, is there an alternative? Solitaire tel un étang dans le soir, au loin, vu par la vitre du train, s'évanouissant si vite dans la pâleur du soir que, même une fois vu, l'étang est à peine arraché à sa solitude. The word order is upended, but you could almost say that translation is a question of word order, of finding the most natural, or rather, most rhythmic order. The least you could say is that this version of the sentence is unsatisfactory; I'll have to return to it.

And the airs return a bit later, the drafts or currents of air have taken possession of time and space, of the house, the novel. It is they and the wind and the roar of the sea that ask the question—but whom are they asking? The furniture that's left, the chairs that can be made out under the sheets covering them, the jugs shrouded with cloth—almost everything is covered, everything is protected (at least appears to be).

"Will you fade? Will you perish?"

Allez-vous pâlir? Allez-vous périr? Or Allez-vous disparaître? Allez-vous périr? For fade, *disparaître* is too long, and *pâlir* would introduce an internal rhyme, a parallel, into the French version that isn't in the English text but might compensate, in a way, for other rhymes or parallelisms that were sacrificed.

As if the question they asked scarcely needed that they should answer: we remain. We remain: *nous restons*. Or *nous demeurons*. Needed—*nécessitaient*. That's debatable, of course, need is more common than necessitate. But what other option is there? Comme si la question qu'ils posaient nécessitait à peine leur réponse : nous demeurons. No: nécessitait à peine qu'ils répondent: nous restons.

Often, a word near the beginning of a sentence is repeated near the end. Like *loveliness* earlier. Or silence in the next sentence now.

Nothing it seemed could break that image, corrupt that innocence, or disturb the swaying mantle of silence, which, week after week, in the empty room, wove into itself the falling cries of birds, ships hooting, the drone and hum of the fields, a dog's bark, a man's shout, and folded them round the house in silence.

The air has a presence, a form, an action. The silence, too. A moment of pure poetry like so many others in "Time Passes." Besides, this sentence remains the same from the typescript to the final version—whether English or American—overcoming all the obstacles, all the rereadings. Even in the very first version, the manuscript, the sentence is there, not in its entirety, but parts of it are taken up, such as *the swaying mantle of silence*, and the corrupted innocence, and *week after week*, which had initially been *day after day*, or the verb *fold*, the *fields*. The *rooks* have become generic birds, and the thunder of the sea has been cut. The manuscript, in the Berg Collection, is the substrate from which the substantially different typescript will develop. The transformations are extensive, much is crossed out or erased, all the characters disappear except for Mrs. McNab, who remains to take note of the effects of abandonment, as once a human silhouette was drawn on an image in order to place a human scale next to enormous buildings, trees, mountains, or giant animals. In the typescript, the descriptions gradually become more like implicit evocations, ghostly, more ephemeral. The text takes flight.

Dresden. Nocturnal landscape. I was looking at a few dug-up streets in the city center, behind fences that allowed glimpses of deep trenches and a vast pit that would accommodate the foundations of a new building. There was still not a soul in sight, except for the ghosts of my life who had apparently arranged to meet here. And yet, not one of them had ever lived in this city, or even passed through it. But perhaps the ghosts prefer to go to places they didn't know, they continue traveling, or they track the steps of those they follow, wherever they lead. Perhaps they saw nothing of Dresden in accompanying me, perhaps they couldn't see. But I was sure they could hear both the sound of my footsteps and my voice—my internal voice—and that they knew I remembered an article I'd recently read on the restitution of bells after the war, the ones that hadn't been melted down, those that had survived and were waiting in the cemetery to rejoin their towers, or, if their origins were unknown or if their native country was on the other side—because the Cold War had just begun—were waiting to be welcomed into a neighboring tower, in a village or a town that was hoping, like a childless couple, to adopt one.

These bells had been given a lovely name. They were called *Patenglocke*—a compound word that joins godparent and bell. There was even an organization charged with restituting the bells, just as there were organizations in charge of restituting works of art. In the count, they distinguished the bells of Protestant churches from those of Catholic churches. There is no indication whether or not this division was respected when the bells were returned, but we can assume it was. There still remained three thousand bells from countries in the Soviet camp, now considered the enemy. The British Military authorities had refused to return the bells to their countries of origin. Hence the bell cemeteries, and, because their storage was becoming too expensive, the decision to distribute them according to the parishes' needs. The restitution campaign was ended in 1953. The bells were considered loans pending any claims. Damaged bells or fragments of bells were given to East Germany so that they could be melted down as compensation for the bells kept by West Germany.

The empty streets became superimposed with black-and-white photographs I'd seen on the Internet of these bells lined up alongside railroad tracks, looking abandoned despite their size, waiting amid the confusion, to be transported according to a strategic plan—adopted after how many hours of discussion? First was Hamburg, the closest city, then Bavaria because all the bells from this federal state could be identified, then the Rhineland. For all the bells that were loaned, or sponsored—like the refugees from the former eastern territories of Germany, Silesia, East Prussia, or the Sudetenland—there was a thirty-year period of protection that ended in the 1980s. What happened to these bells? Were they able to stay in their adoptive churches or did they have to emigrate once again? Did the bells of the requiem played in Dresden come from elsewhere and if so, from which cities?

I sensed the river's presence. At night, the water gains a moving solidity, especially near the dusky streets. I thought of the Dickens novel I'd read shortly before coming to Dresden that begins with a description of boats floating on the Thames, keeping a lookout for corpses of the drowned which might have money on them. All nocturnal waters have something of the Styx about them and carry within them, visible or invisible, the boat of the dead. Instead of continuing along the street to the terraces overlooking the Elbe and turning to climb the steps leading to the door in the majestic edifice that was in such contrast to the simplicity of my room within, I branched off to the right to reach the riverbank. I had to cross a major road. Now and again, the glare of headlights and the sound of a motor swept over me, but I was on the side of the water, my back turned to the domes that formed the contours of the city—even in the paintings by Canaletto, who lived in Dresden for eleven years—looking at the other bank where ancient palaces displayed their architecture. I liked the grass that had been left on the opposite bank as an intermediary zone between river and city to lessen the risk of flooding and in the night—although there was no sign of the moon—I could make out the presence of this space at once empty and inhabited, favorable to ephemeral forms.

Why, at that moment, did I think of the legend of Aristaeus, as recounted by Virgil in the fourth book of the *Georgics*? Perhaps because it describes the subterranean space that is both the gods' retreat and the source of the great rivers that rise from underground and flow over the earth's surface. The Elbe is not included in the names listed, as are the Tiber, the Phasis, and the Po. Virgilian geography did not extend to Germania, but under the dim lights of the opposite bank, the Elbe could well have been born in that underground realm and secretly carried the mysteries from below. The infrequent but regular sound of passing cars created a low rumbling like that of the sea and, despite the presence of another riverbank, more ghostly than real, I imagined I was on an ocean shore. The legend of Aristaeus as recounted by Virgil. The loss of his bees to a sudden and mysterious death. Aristaeus weeps at the source of the stream where his mother, a nymph, lives. She opens the gates to her subterranean aquatic realm for him. She suggests they pour a libation to Ocean. Then Aristaeus will have to seize Proteus, who roams ports and seas, for Proteus knows the secrets of time and will be able to tell him why his bees died. It's no small paradox that the key to the bees' secret is to be found in the watery realm, not the airy one. Aristaeus is able to capture Proteus. The latter complies with Aristaeus's demand, grudgingly at first and then willingly. He tells the story of Orpheus, who descended to the Underworld in search of Eurydice. Eurydice was leading the nymphs in dance and died fleeing a swarm of bees. The nymphs took revenge by killing all the bees. In exchange for offerings and prayers, Proteus says, the nymphs of the valleys will forgive you. Aristaeus follows Proteus's instructions. His offerings include poppies, which sow forgetting. The rotten flesh of sacrificed cattle, Virgil's book tells us, liberates the bees and the swarm flies up to the treetops. I imagined the spot where Aristaeus wept to be like the other bank of the Elbe with its ghostly palaces. And I thought of *Silent Spring*, Rachel Carson's book from the early sixties, which opens with the gripping scene of a landscape without a single birdsong, a mute world. I thought of bees today and their disappearance, the cause of which, like that of the birds in Carson's book, was less poetic than the nymphs' revenge, unless the nymphs are also avenging the spread of pesticides.

Then again peace descended; and the shadow wavered; light bent to its own image in adoration on the bedroom wall; when Mrs. McNab, tearing the veil of silence with hands that had stood in the wash-tub, grinding it with boots that had crunched the shingle, came as directed to open all windows and dust the bedrooms.

Someone comes and disturbs the barely restored silence. Mrs. McNab has come to clean, *as directed*. The Ramsay family is grouped into this past participle, whereas everything Mrs. McNab does is described externally, as if observed by the house and what constitutes it.

Then again peace descended—again because in the preceding sentence a board had creaked, *as after centuries of quiescence, a rock rends itself from the mountain and hurtles crashing into the valley.*

Puis la paix redescendit; et l'ombre vacilla; la lumière s'inclina vers sa propre image en adoration sur le mur de la chambre. Or Au mur de la chambre? Is the image in adoration of the light or the light in adoration of the image? quand Mrs. McNab, déchirant le voile du silence avec des mains qui s'étaient trouvées dans le bac à lessive, avec des mains qui avaient trempé dans la bassine, or avec des mains ayant lavé le linge—no, hands that had done the washing is too abstract for the *wash-tub,* which in English we immediately see in its matter and form—l'écrasant avec des bottes qui avaient crissé sur les galets. What precautions and detours are necessary to render the *boots that had crunched the shingle* in French, it's not working . . . *came as directed*, vint comme demandé pour ouvrir toutes les fenêtres et nettoyer les chambres.

I'll have to rework everything to find the poetic simplicity of the English. . . . l'écrasant sous ses bottes qui avaient crissé sur les galets, vint comme on le lui avait demandé ouvrir toutes les fenêtres et nettoyer les chambres. That's better, but maybe I should write l'écrasant sous des bottes qui avaient crissé, and I should check the punctuation. I can't keep the semicolon after the bedroom wall, because the clause in which Mrs. McNab emerges is subordinate to the one in which the light appears.

So ends Chapter Four, if we can call these brief numbered moments chapters. Chapter Five is entirely dedicated to Mrs.

McNab's cleaning, to her movements and gestures described from an indeterminate point of view. As if the objects in the house were fixing their attention—we hardly dare call it their gaze—on her.

"Sometimes, on Sundays, I heard bells," Thoreau writes in *Walden.* Then he describes the sound that comes from a distance, four bells from four different locations, Lincoln, Acton, Bedford, or Concord, acquiring through the woods a certain hum, a natural melody, the vibration of the universal lyre, he writes, as if every leaf and needle of the wood had contributed to it. A natural melody . . . And yet, there was a world that didn't know this melody; the melody's beginning is something no one can establish. There's some consensus about its literary origin, which is a medieval romance from the thirteenth century—*Le Haut Libre du Graal*, better known as *Perlesvaus*, or *Perceval.* This narrative recounts the events that occurred leading up to and following Chrétien de Troyes's *Perceval*, and focuses not only on Perceval's adventures but also those of King Arthur and the knights Lancelot and Gawain. Late in the romance—the story branches into several strands—in Book 9 (of 11), the one in which Arthur, Lancelot, and Gawain are reunited, the three of them take refuge in the middle of the forest in the house of a young woman. Every night, demonic knights attack the house, which is protected only by a circle she traces with a sword. When the demons appear with their fiery lances, Lancelot charges at them, followed by Arthur and Gawain. They defeat the first horde, but another appears. "As their furious battle reached its highest pitch, they heard the tolling of a bell in the forest, and the fiendish knights immediately gave up the fight and fled." The lady told them that she heard the bell every night and that is what saves her.

"Joséphès tells us that, in this era, there were as yet no bells in Great Britain or Britannia Inferior, and that people were summoned with a horn; in some parts, there were only metal drums, and in others wooden rattles. King Arthur was astonished by so beautiful and harmonious a sound. It seemed to him that it must come from a divine source and that it would be an excellent thing, if possible, to see what had produced it." In Book 10, three hermits come to see King Arthur in the castle conquered by Perceval. One of them wears a bell around his neck, and this hermit, a king converted to the "New Law" who had also converted his subjects, tells Arthur that, one morning, in a solitary hermitage on the seashore, he saw a boat land. There were three priests on board who told him that Solomon had had three bells forged "in honor of the Savior of the World, his gentle mother, and the saints." The priests had brought one of them (as the Grail had been brought from Holy Land) "to this island because it had none." The bell would serve as a model "for all those that would be built in its image in this island kingdom, where none have yet existed." King Arthur recognized the sound of the bell that had saved him and his knights in their adventure recounted in Book 9. This is how bells came to Great Britain and to literature.

The sound of bells from an evening requiem had long since faded away the night I stood indecisively on the bank of the

Elbe, lost in time and space, looking at the other shore. My thoughts whirled, names and places, memories that belonged to me and memories that didn't. It was as if the city had visited me, especially its shadows—I mean, shades of people from the past, all those from the circles of the Romantics who had gathered here, as well as those who had come seeking refuge, and those who had fled, the ephemeral residents—as if the centuries had come together here on the bank of the Elbe. I had the sense that I was on the verge of understanding something, but what? Here, one bent over the city's mystery, its former glory, the decline it had suffered after the fall of the Wall and the disappearance of the country it had been part of, the German Democratic Republic. And the anti-immigrant group that had been formed in Dresden, and was growing ever larger, gathered every week to demonstrate against foreigners. Recently, a political party took their lead and has gained even more influence. That night on the river's edge, I recalled a concert announcement I'd seen in Paris in 1990 or 1991. I'd noted the name of the orchestra, the Staatskapelle Dresden, an historic orchestra of the city of Dresden, founded in 1548, I'd read somewhere in town recently, and I remembered thinking of it as an orchestra from a country that no longer exists . . . Everything endures in one form or another, and the vanished country lives on as a phantom in the recreated land. Just as those I've lost have left something of themselves in me that doesn't belong to me and yet is a part of me at the same time as they hover somewhere between earth and water as vague forms of hope or sorrow.

—But one shouldn't trust appearances or believe in a return of wilderness.

—In the days following the Chernobyl disaster, bodies of dead animals were strewn over the ground. The plants, flowers, and insects—even the grass—everything looked different. And there was no one left—135,000 people had been evacuated.

—Cesium closely resembles calcium, and strontium resembles potassium. Both isotopes were absorbed by the plants and animals in the place of calcium and potassium, which can no longer be found in the exclusion zone. The bones of the animals there have a high concentration of cesium, not calcium.

—And so, life thrives and multiplies on foundations that should not exist. Everything appears normal, but the reality is different. The apparently healthy animals we see in the documentaries are aliens. A parallel world has been created, a temporal fracture.

INTERLUDE

The High Line on an autumn evening when the city's lights go on. The transparence of glass and the tracery of steel girders create an unreal backdrop that wavers between construction site and science-fiction film. Is it the future we pass through on this long promenade? Do the apartments overlooking the walkway of exotic hardwood planking house the people of the future? Will the future be filled with these warm shades of yellow and brown? Does it consist only of luxury design objects? On the promenade in the evening, you have the feeling of going from one apartment to the next, from neighbor to neighbor through large, well-lit rooms—all of them empty. Passing through tunnels, in the shade, where the history of the railway line originated; bypassing, branching off, approaching the tracks, or seeing them disappear or covered with wild plants that were not otherwise destined to find shelter there . . . The High Line has come to signify that nothing lasts, not even what seems eternally fixed—by the measure of a human life, things may seem to last and structures to take root, but one or two generations are enough for everything to disappear, for what had seemed self-evident to become doubtful, for what had seemed unimaginable to occur, and for the past to return transformed into the future.

In the distance is the Hudson River, a large fluid, maritime expanse; the wind blows over the High Line and the waterway is ruffled, waves form, memories surface of large ocean liners it once welcomed on Pier 54, where survivors of the *Titanic* docked on the *Carpathia* . . . This steamship, built in England for the Cunard Line, was launched in 1902 and made one or two modest trial runs from one river to another before sailing between Liverpool and Boston a year later and then from New York City to southern waters. The Atlantic in the summer, the Mediterranean in winter: this was its schedule. But one night, the *Carpathia*'s wireless operator, when listening to the messages he had missed when he was on the bridge, heard a distress signal. The *Titanic* had just struck an iceberg and was requesting help. She was a hundred kilometers away and the *Carpathia* changed course to meet her. It took three and a half hours. During this time, the public rooms on the ship were transformed into a hospital, an improvised emergency room. The ice slowed its progress, and the *Carpathia* arrived an hour and a half after the *Titanic* had sunk. One thousand five hundred passengers disappeared in the water, but 700 survived, and were transferred from the lifeboats onto the *Carpathia* over the next four and a half hours. After some hesitation, the *Carpathia* returned to New York and reached the port, Pier 54, the evening of April 18, 1912. Four days after the shipwreck. The captain was knighted by King George V, crew members were covered with medals, and the *Carpathia* continued her career as an ocean liner until the First World War, during which it transported American and Canadian troops to Great Britain. Her illustrious career ended when she was torpedoed by a German submarine in 1918, off the southwest tip of England. Five dead and 213 survivors—the *Carpathia's* story is one of survival, which did not end with her sinking because, after several mistaken identifications, the wreck was found at a depth of 150 meters.

Ships no longer dock at Pier 54, only a metal arch testifies to its past. But on the High Line at night, when the windows of the apartments have gone dark and all those strolling have dispersed, maybe one of the survivors reappears on the boards that recall the deck of the transatlantic liner on which he made the crossing from Europe to America, maybe one of those who vanished at sea finally reaches his port of arrival, this longed-for New York, and now wanders up and down every night, contemplating the port he could not reach when alive along with its mysterious arch that seems to open onto infinity . . .

For thirty years, this disused site was abandoned to nature and, as in the Chernobyl exclusion zone, the vegetation proliferated, not only native species but also others come from afar, transported by the trains of long ago, dropped from the soles of those who ventured onto the site, or by birds, or by the wind . . . In 2000, far from the celebrations of the future and the new age of technology, the Friends of the High Line asked Joel Sternfeld to photograph the abandoned tracks. Sternfeld discovered a space worthy of the expanses in the American West—those designated as "wilderness," a concept and word that doesn't really exist in French. And yet, there are places in France that could claim this designation, not so much in the surface area, in square kilometers, as in the impression they give, the views they offer, the freedom of undeveloped spaces. The photographer explained that he only shot under gray skies; he thought of William Henry Jackson, who had been given a commission to open up the Rocky Mountains and Yellowstone to those who could not travel there, to display this West that was unknown to the rest of the United States. The photographs he brought back greatly contributed to the classification of Yellowstone as a national park. "We have become great because of the lavish use of our resources. But the time has come to inquire seriously what will happen when our forests are gone, when the coal, the iron, the oil, and the gas are exhausted, when the soils have still further impoverished and washed into the streams, polluting the rivers, denuding the fields and obstructing navigation," Theodor Roosevelt wrote before becoming president in 1901. He would use his presidency to conserve great tracts of natural land and to protect archeological sites.

On overcast days, in Joel Sternfeld's images, the grass is yellow or the ground soggy, hardened snow has accumulated between the rails and outside them, sparse grass struggles to overcome the stones, or a fruit tree struggles to survive. It's yellow, white, gray and the buildings in the distance, large, abandoned cubes, form the only verticals in the landscape. Today, the green of the renewed gardens and the colors of the flowers tell another story, the intrinsic contrast of a garden that appears natural. Nature recreated, but with an apparent wildness. At night, under LED lights at ground level, the vegetation takes on a supernatural air, aquatic plants and plants native to the prairies share the space, come from all over the United States, sometimes from Europe or Asia . . . Curtains of rough horsetail, tall, evergreen stems—a little like bamboo—that, in Japan, are boiled and dried to use as sandpaper or to smooth clarinet reeds . . . Forest plants, lesser calamint, the High Line is a miniature universe, to be sure, you have to walk through it, but you also have to stop, bend down, observe. The remains of wooden piles that supported the piers form another kind of forest visible from a distance. They look like the backs of whales or dolphins, dark-colored marine creatures, now grouped together, now dispersed, aquatic fauna responding to the vegetation above and moving in the current and the wake of passing boats.

III

A kind of presence, a soul, stirred around me, a light breeze, the Elbe rose with a gentle swell, someone had come to see me, wanted to speak to me, a voice, a shape—the offshoot of dead stars, of vanished orbs? I pictured the monument, the black obelisk floated on the water, drifted upstream toward the source, while the clouds in the sky prevented any reading of the stars. Only a crescent moon was visible for a moment before immediately melting into the cloudy mass. *Gone over.* The words from Michael Powell's film returned to me, the simple stone on the edge of the cliff with the engraving *Peter Manson, gone over.* At sea, one doesn't die, one disappears. But Peter Manson didn't die at sea, he had tried to scale the cliff using a rope that he knew would fray at the very spot where his son had competed with Andrew, the man now returning to Foula on a sailboat. I had the dramatic images of the fall in mind, I could almost see it in the waters of the Elbe, calm as they were. The ocean bordering the island was not very rough that day, but the fall was fatal. The stone Andrew discovers ten years later . . . A name—those names engraved in stone, in memory, in the heart . . . sometimes that's all that's left of someone and so much effort is often required to identify anonymous corpses and give them back the name refused them by the death they'd had to suffer, a name instead of a gravestone, a name to serve as a gravestone . . . *Gone over.* Missing, departed. Overboard. From one shore to the other. From the shore of the living to the shore of the dead. The river's water erased their features, who could know, even fleetingly, what was happening inside another—all my life I'd been confronted with the desire, the impossibility, of fusing with another . . .

That night in Dresden, without hearing the bells of the requiem and without seeing any names engraved in stone, that night I hardly slept. Back in my room, thinking I was tired, I had lain down with the window open despite the cold to hear the murmur of the city and to soften the sense of loneliness which had suddenly overcome me and made me turn back, reach for the heavy key in my pocket—the kind of key it's hard to imagine still exists—then fumble in the dark for the keyhole to insert the key, climb the stairs to the third floor: all automatic gestures that seemed to have acquired a meaning at night, or rather, a goal. Was this goal to forget the name that had hounded me all the way back and made me leave the riverbank because its letters held so much pain? Closing my eyes in the city's murmur, did I think that there would be less risk of dreaming, that is, of dreaming about it?

The spring without a leaf to toss, bare and bright like a virgin fierce in her chastity, scornful in her purity, was laid out on fields wide-eyed and watchful and entirely careless of what was done or thought by the beholders.

What an odd image, spring like a fierce virgin.

Le printemps sans une feuille à jeter, nu, éclatant comme une vierge farouche dans sa chasteté, méprisante dans sa pureté, s'étendait sur les champs les yeux grands ouverts, vigilant, se moquant totalement de ce qui était fait ou pensé par les spectateurs. Another failure. Another sentence that doesn't fit. This passive voice excludes humans, or rather, gives them a secondary role. It's the spring that acts, it's spring that counts. I have to try again, from the top. How can it be done? These *beholders*, how can I bring them in without sounding ponderous? Le printemps sans feuille à arracher, lumineux et nu comme une vierge farouche par sa chasteté, méprisante par sa pureté, s'étalait sur les champs avec candeur (taking wide-eyed figuratively and not in the literal sense of "eyes wide open"), s'étalait sur les champs avec candeur, vigilance, se moquant totalement de ce que les spectateurs faisaient ou pensaient. It's getting better, but it's still not right. The sentence should end with the beholders, the *spectateurs*, because someone does appear in the next sentence—in brackets.

I had a daily routine. In the morning, I'd go out for breakfast—the guesthouse I was staying in didn't offer any. I would walk through the still-empty streets, skirting a construction site and arriving at the large square where groups of tourists would gather a bit later and listen to a guide tell them the history of the Frauenkirche, the church that is now a symbol of reconciliation, rebuilt thanks to donations from, among other places, Great Britain, erasing Coventry, or rather the spirit of revenge. The building's black stones are those that had been left in a pile of rubble as a site of commemoration in the GDR, and many would have preferred to leave them that way instead of building a new church. The white stones are from today. It is true that the collapsed facade and the pile of stones that resembled a petrified waterfall offered an impressive and concrete image of war's devastation. Paradoxically, however, conserving the ruins was so costly that they decided to rebuild. Continuing on my way, I came to another square, much larger and lined with more recent buildings that, in winter, faced the Christmas market, and finally I reached the majestic Kultur-palast. This cultural center, a cubic building of glass on pillars, at once solid and fragile, all transparence and light, houses a library and a concert hall, and in the foyer is a café entirely of glass where the administrators, musicians, librarians, and passersby meet for work or conversation depending on the time of day. There, I would order a hot drink and rolls or muesli, but more importantly, I'd collect treasures of life and light that helped inspire courage to make it through the day and my desire to work. I'd bring my laptop and measure the rhythm of Woolfian sentences against the city's movement.

[*Prue Ramsay, leaning on her father's arm, was given in marriage that May. What, people said, could have been more fitting. And, they added, how beautiful she looked!*]

So many possibilities, even for such a simple phrase. For example, Prue Ramsay, au bras de son père, on her father's arm, but then we lose *leaning*—appuyée, s'appuyant, penchée—was given in marriage, always this active-passive tense, so to speak, when it comes to human figures, ce mois de mai, en mai, that month of May, in May. Quoi de plus adapté, disaient les gens. Comment pourrait-on rêver mieux, disaient les gens, what could have been more fitting, people said. Could anything have been more fitting, people said. *And, they added*—but to whom are they speaking? Is it Mrs. McNab who is being told the news, or are these comments made on the wedding day?—*how beautiful she looked!* Prue is being looked at, a purely external scene in which there is no certainty, just echoes and impressions—it's not that she is beautiful, but that others see her and find her beautiful. So in French this could be: Prue Ramsay, conduite au bras de son père (to respect the rhythm and the image, even if the meaning is slightly changed), fut donnée en mariage en mai, fut mariée en mai, was given in marriage in May, was married in May. Or perhaps, Comment rêver mieux, disaient les gens. Ils ajoutaient, et comme elle était belle! You couldn't dream of anything better, people said. And, they added, how beautiful she was!

Death, illness, marriage, children, everything occurs in brackets. Don't we also behave this way, pushing the most difficult events to the margins of our awareness? Going about our business automatically, mechanically. This translation, I thought to myself as I looked out of the café window at the tramcars stopping and dropping off their cargo of passengers, passing each other, then departing, gliding silently in the direction of the Elbe or the train station, crossing the city as mysteriously as the sailboat returning from the open sea glimpsed through the rock arch on the island shore in Michael Powell's film, this translation was helping me forget—momentarily—

the loss I had come here to erase through distance and work. Even if the work—because *To the Lighthouse* is infused with life, and its various phases, of which mourning is one, of course, as are the journey, encounters, and difficulties in life, not to mention the locations, the light, the sea—even if the work led me back to the heart of this loss, often when I expected it the least, with a single word, an image.

After breakfast, I would open the book and my laptop and settle myself by the sea, next to the window, at the city's edge, moving from screen to page, from page to screen, from one era to another, one language to another. Or I would walk back to my room and its silence along the same streets, now slightly busier, but I returned less frequently. The longer I extended my stay, the more often I spent mornings in the café, interrupting the day with a walk along the river, before getting back to my translation in the afternoon in the solitude of my room—which occasionally felt burdensome—and going out again in the evening, sometimes crossing one of the large bridges to immerse myself in the noise of the cafés and popular restaurants that revealed another side of the city.

—In Píšt', a small town in the Czech Republic near the Polish border, formerly part of Upper Silesia, a region that was once part of Germany, a man set out in search of the historic bell of the Saint Lawrence Church, built in 1743. He finally traced it to a village in the Black Forest, on the Neckar, the river that Hölderlin could see from his tower.

—The Upper Silesian Church is Catholic, the one on the Neckar River Protestant.

—In Sulz—this is the name of the German village—the church had been rebuilt after the war, and because the original bell-tower had burned down, they welcomed the exiled bell.

—The first letter the pastor received asked if his church's bell did, in fact, come from Píšt' as indicated by records in the archives of the Nuremberg Museum, an institution dedicated to the history and registration of bells. The pastor was not particularly pleased. Returning the bell would require demolishing the tower to extract it, then rebuilding the tower and having a new bell made.

—The diocese nonetheless approved restitution of the bell. The cost was estimated at 100,000 euros and lawyers began drawing up a contract between the two parishes.

—The region of Píšt' is a complicated one. The border with Poland shifted over time; it even cut through towns and separated the residents.

—The Saint Lawrence Church is dedicated to pilgrimage and reconciliation, to harmony between peoples. Píšt' is well placed to understand the importance of this. Finally, it was decided that the bells would stay where they were, that beyond national affiliation and borders, sound would symbolize unity—when the bell from Píšt' rang in Sulz, its echo would be heard, in a sense, in Píšt'.

—And so, a second letter waiving restitution arrived in Sulz. The residents of Sulz took note—with astonishment, perhaps, but nothing else.

—In Píšt', however, a plaque was made recounting the history of the bell in both Czech and German. Then a video of the full church on the day of the plaque's unveiling was sent to Sulz.

—This time, the community of Sulz was moved by the depth of engagement, by the many people who came together and agreed to let the community of Sulz keep their bell. There was even talk of some parishioners from Sulz visiting the parish of Píšt'.

What is private in the loss of someone close? What is personal, what is collective? What can be shared? Should we keep our memories to ourselves, or must they, can they even be told? Will what each person says turn off onto a different path, then rejoin what others have said, or will these separate paths run parallel forever? I remembered conversations, moments, smiles, expressions, intonations, but all these don't make a person, at most they constitute a memory, and from now on I would have to live with these fragments and try to shape them into an image. I wasn't aware, before, of the confidence it takes to buy a book, for example, and place it on your bookshelf, saying, I'll keep it for later, or to start to read then put it aside, sensing that the time isn't right. What confidence it takes to say to yourself, later. To think that it will be possible. That it won't be too late. And so, not to wonder each time, when seeing someone now and again, if there will be another time. To believe in continuity. To agree to meet three weeks in advance, to plan a trip, everything we do without a second thought. Then one day, someone disappears, and we are filled with regret. If we'd seen each other more often, if we'd known, if this or that sentence, instead of falling on deaf ears or being left unsaid, had been taken up, answered, judged according to its value? If this or that answer had sounded differently? What we keep, what we remember, what's there without our knowing and may emerge one day—what is lost forever. Would he have known, would she have known, what they meant to us, how much they counted? And this place, now left empty, what to do with it?

As the summer neared, as the evenings lengthened, there came to the wakeful, the hopeful, walking the beach, stirring the pool, imaginations of the strangest kind—of flesh turned to atoms which drove before the wind, of stars flashing in their hearts, of cliff, sea, cloud, and sky brought purposely together to assemble outwardly the scattered parts of the vision within.

Tandis que l'été approchait, que les soirées rallongeaient, vinrent chez ceux demeurés éveillés, pleins d'espoir, qui marchaient sur la plage, ou remuaient l'étang, les visions les plus étranges – chair transformée en atomes et chassée par le vent, étoiles qui luisaient en leur cœur, falaise, mer, nuage et ciel recueillis à dessein ensemble pour rassembler à l'extérieur les éclats dispersés d'une vision intérieure . . . But using vision for imaginations and again for vision won't work. Images, maybe? . . . Tandis que l'été approchait, que les soirées rallongeaient, surgirent en ceux demeurés (or restés ?) éveillés, pleins d'espoir, marchant sur la plage ou remuant l'étang, les images les plus étranges—chair transformée en atomes et chassée par le vent, étoiles luisant en leur cœur, falaise, mer, nuage et ciel recueillis à dessein pour rassembler à l'extérieur les éclats dispersés d'une vision intérieure.

The peaceful walk on the beach, nights of insomnia or simply staying up late stand in contrast to the dispersed atoms of flesh, the war flashing again through the thoughts of the peaceful, peaceable strollers on seashore. On the English coast, you could occasionally hear explosions of shells on the shores of France and this pulverized hopes for peace. But some people continued to walk the beach, still hopeful.

In those mirrors, the minds of men, in those pools of uneasy water, in which clouds for ever turn and shadows form, dreams persisted, and it was impossible to resist the strange intimation which every gull, flower, tree, man and woman, and the white earth itself seemed to declare (but if questioned at once to withdraw) that good triumphs, happiness prevails, order rules;

The sentence continues after the semicolon, but this passage is already dense enough. It's extraordinary how everything develops, first as a vision, or rather a flash, then as a persistent image. The *pools of uneasy water* come directly from the pools being stirred in the previous sentence, the *clouds* that reappear, the *imaginations* that develop or deteriorate into *shadows, dreams, the strange intimations* echoing the *imaginations of the strangest kind.*

So then . . . Dans ces miroirs, les esprits des hommes, dans ces étangs d'eau malaisée—a literal translation is rarely satisfying, but it's a necessary first step—dans lesquels les nuages apparaissent à jamais et les ombres se forment, les rêves persistaient et il était impossible de résister à l'étrange sentiment que chaque mouette, fleur, arbre, homme et femme, et la blanche terre elle-même semblaient énoncer (mais étant questionnés, retiraient aussitôt), que le bien triomphe, que le bonheur prévaut, que l'ordre règne. What a thicket. You need to move the branches aside, to enter, to push your way through it. Maybe even prune it? Dans le miroir qu'est l'esprit des hommes, in the mirror that is the mind of men—that plural is important, it has to be kept. And too bad if you have to add a verb, it's not so bad; it simply works as a connector in the sentence even if, in English, minds are contrasted to mirrors. Dans les miroirs que sont les esprits des hommes, dans les étangs d'eau inquiète où apparaissent à jamais les nuages, où se forment les ombres, les rêves persistaient et il était impossible de résister à l'étrange déclaration que chaque mouette, et fleur, arbre, homme ou femme, jusqu'à la terre blanche semblait faire (aussitôt retirée au moindre questionnement), le bien triomphe, le bonheur a cours et l'ordre règne.

What a beautiful way of representing the impossible striving for peace, the negation of troubling events that occur—a war, a loss, some misfortune. What lies we tell ourselves when we repeat phrases like "everything is fine," "everything's still as it was."

I contemplated being immersed in loss as entering water, not gradually as on a beach but abruptly as from a lakefront. You walk away from shore on what seems to be a gentle downward slope and suddenly the water is up to your chest. A few more steps and you've lost your footing. To be submerged in loss, to measure its unexpected depth, astonishing and unfathomable. Not to take its measure, but to realize that it has none, that it is a constant companion, the faithful shadow that follows you, waiting for an opportunity to take hold of you, that it is both friend and enemy, that it won't leave you in peace.

In that café with large glass windows, through which light flooded even on overcast days, even on rainy days, that café in which she'd never stepped foot because she had never been in Dresden I believe, I saw her, or rather, I saw something—someone?—a presence, something impalpable, difficult to discern and identify but part of us nonetheless, part of our idea of the world. Aside from our conversations, there was her writing, which had, book by book, become lodged within me over the years, even though I couldn't have exactly quoted any of it. It was embedded somewhere inside me, like a Sleeping Beauty waiting to be awakened. And occasionally it did wake, unexpectedly, adding a scene that was written, composed, or dreamed to a scene I was living. A friend, a soul, sorrow, someone who wrote whereas I translated, I tried to render a voice as exactly as possible while she tried to find her own way of expressing things that both resembled and did not resemble what she was; it wasn't easy to describe; it was something she worked on that was, at the same time, beyond her. If I were to say that writing took hold of her, I would be misrepresenting the process or rather of my sense of it. I knew nothing about it and neither, if we are to believe her, did she. Still, she worked conscientiously and what she read and wrote both reflected her high idea of literature and contributed to it.

In the café with the large glass windows, into which the light shone despite the thick layer of clouds, one day when the sense of loss was particularly intense, I came upon a sentence in my translation that evoked springtime.

Moreover, softened and acquiescent, the spring with her bees humming and gnats dancing threw her cloak about her, veiled her eyes, averted her head, and among passing shadows and flights of small rain seemed to have taken upon her a knowledge of the sorrows of mankind.

My first question was what to do with that feminine pronoun, that *her*, that pops up unexpectedly. Did I miss the arrival of some woman? It was as if the friend I'd been thinking of had just appeared, as if she'd left traces in the text or as if the text had conjured her through anticipation. But no woman is mentioned before this sentence. So who, what—which presence? The feminine pronoun jumped out at me. Did it refer to spring? To *La primavera*? The young woman in a garden in Botticelli's painting? Moreover, because spring—if that's what "she" refers to—is masculine in French, *le printemps*, I'd have to put *softened and acquiescent* and all the rest in the masculine form, unless I used *la primavera*, which would add an element of sophistication completely foreign to Woolf's text. . . . et ses abeilles qui bourdonnent et ses moucherons qui dansent se drapait dans sa cape, voilait son regard, détournait la tête, et parmi les ombres qui passaient et les brèves averses de pluie, semblait avoir pris en charge la connaissance des chagrins de l'humanité. Pris en charge, taken charge of, is going a bit far for *to have taken upon her*, but it's one way to avoid determining gender, because in French possessive adjectives don't indicate the gender of the possessor but only that of the object possessed. Avait pris sur soi? No, that could be confusing. Et ses abeilles bourdonnantes et ses moucherons dansants? Et ses abeilles qui bourdonnaient, ses moucherons qui dansaient? Et le bourdonnement des abeilles et la danse des moucherons? And her humming bees and dancing gnats? And her bees that hummed, her gnats that danced? And the humming of the bees and the dance of the gnats? Each of these possibilities hid an attempt to forget. I clung to the text that unfolded smoothly before me—Woolf's, that is, not my translation—to save myself, to escape the lake that, contrary to all logic, was flooding the land.

Occasionally I had a vision of—how can I describe it—a bubble coming out of someone, the way the genie is drawn escaping from Aladdin's lamp in books, a creature with an external life of its own that nonetheless came from the lamp. Sometimes, when listening to this friend talk about her work, or especially when reading her writing, I had the sense of a creature that had escaped her thoughts, her body, escaped from inside her and was growing larger and larger like the genie from the lamp, until it takes on a shape and life of its own. I never told her about this vision; I probably couldn't have described it clearly and maybe I hadn't even had it yet. It's not that the thoughts expressed in her books contradicted those she expressed in her life; I recognized it all, down to the voice, but there was something else, come from elsewhere, who knows where, an unidentified object that took over the text and turned it into something other than a simple extension of its author.

—Slavutych is a city like any other. Like any other? Not exactly. Designed to relocate the residents evacuated from Pripyat, it was built in 1986 and was inhabitable two years later.

—The idea was to make it a twenty-first-century model city, just as Pripyat had been a model in its time—all those model cities that collapse one day.

—The city is divided into eight districts named after the capitals of former Soviet republics—which still existed, although only for a short while—capitals from the eight lands of the Soviet Union that contributed to the city's construction.

—Slavutych is located on the edge of the exclusion zone, a strange city with monuments, a forest, statues, an angel. A museum with a reconstructed apartment from Pripyat in the 1980s. Pedestrian zones, cement, trees.

—A city. Twenty-five thousand residents in the middle of the forest—an oversized city, inhabited but still a ghost town. Stadiums, lawns, apartment blocks, birch trees, fir trees, arteries built for residents who never came.

—The real inhabitants are probably the statues, the memorials, the faces sculpted in marble, the liquidators, the dead of Chernobyl, the heroes.

—The playgrounds in the parks remain empty.

—Which city will house a museum with a reconstructed apartment from Slavutych in the 2010s?

Here are the brackets again, the loss for which *the sorrows of mankind* prepared us.

[*Prue Ramsay died that summer in some illness connected with childbirth, which was indeed a tragedy, people said. They said nobody deserved happiness more.*]

An apparent indifference. Indifference? Apparent? Prue? Wasn't she the one who had just been given in marriage on her father's arm a page before? The one who looked so beautiful? Time passes; it passes with all that it contains. At first glance, these two sentences look easy, but they have a certain number of traps. Should *connected with childbirth* be liée à la naissance d'un enfant or liée à un accouchement? But *accouchement* won't work unless it it's *son accouchement*. However, there's no pronoun in the English, nothing to indicate possession or the person; everything is impersonal, *people said, they said*. Ils disaient que personne ne méritait davantage le bonheur. Or rather Ils disaient que personne ne méritait autant d'être heureux. That's better. But the first sentence is tricky. Prue Ramsay mourut cet été d'une maladie (it's best to add the qualifier *quelconque* for *some*) d'une quelconque maladie due à un accouchement. No, take out *quelconque*. Prue Ramsay mourut cet été d'une maladie liée, provoquée par un accouchement, ce qui était une tragédie, vraiment, dirent les gens. Ils dirent que personne ne méritait autant d'être heureux. Ils disaient? Ils dirent? Imperfect or simple past?

In these brackets, nothing should stick out; everything should be as even as the beach on which people seeking an answer walk in the evening. Prue Ramsay mourut cet été-là d'une maladie provoquée par un accouchement, ce qui était une réelle tragédie, disaient les gens. Ils disaient que personne ne méritait autant d'être heureux. In French, the imperfect is definitely less obtrusive than the simple past.

I had gone to see the shades—was theirs a realm or a village? The streets were winding and narrow; the buildings were protected by high walls, but sometimes, thanks to a grille or an open gate, you could catch a glimpse of the modest or vast residences—because the shades aren't alike—walls covered with ivy or vines, and grassy lawns. Fruit trees generously offered their laden branches to passersby. But the streets were empty; the shades did not emerge until nighttime, when they wouldn't be seen, avoiding the streetlamps, even the dim lights, advancing with silent steps. I was only passing through. Each newcomer to this village or realm probably believes he or she is only passing through, but wasn't this the best proof of the fact that I had returned from it as mysteriously as I had arrived there? This wasn't a dream or a vision—but something of a different order. The village had perhaps slipped between the pages of a book, perhaps it had arisen from a sentence. In any case, it had suddenly appeared, and I recognized her in one of the shades because, despite the darkness, I could distinguish forms and, although I heard no voices, certain names came to me, and each name settled on a form, making the shades complete—because shades are not made for anonymity—and among them was hers.

And now in the heat of summer the wind sent its spies about the house again.

The rhythm of the sentence. *And now*. Et maintenant, too long. Or just maintenant. Maintenant, dans la chaleur de l'été, le vent renvoyait ses espions aux abords de la maison. And here begins the vision that announces, describes, evokes across the years, what will happen fifty years later, farther to the east of the island with this house and from which the lighthouse was visible.

Flies wove a web in the sunny rooms; weeds that had grown close to the glass in the night tapped methodically at the window pane.

It seems best to use the pluperfect here. Des mouches avaient tissé une toile (leur toile?) dans les pièces ensoleillées; des herbes ou plutôt, de mauvaises herbes ayant poussé près de la vitre dans la nuit. A web or their web? And in the night—is it that the weeds grew in the night or that they tapped at the window in the night? Flies—when you'd expect spiders. Is this because spider has two syllables but flies only one and the sentence is composed almost entirely of monosyllables? *Heat, wind, spies* and the internal rhyme flies/spies—anything is possible . . . I checked, the sentence made it through all the editions intact: English, American, first, second, uniform. This wasn't completely true. There was the treasure, the inestimable goldmine under the name of The Berg Collection. The manuscript full of corrections, some pages with only a few lines, difficult to decipher when the writing was rushed, but under the cursor the magic of digitalization turns the handwriting into print letters. This original, manuscript version differs noticeably from the typescript, which is misleadingly labeled "proofs" on the website that generously makes the different versions of *To the Lighthouse* accessible online. At first, I thought this meant the publisher's proofs, but in fact it's an intermediate version between the manuscript and the first English edition, called a typescript. In the original version, aside from the fact that it is in springtime rather than the heat of summer, there was a list—*flies, gnats, spiders*—later crossed out. The gnats were moved to an earlier sentence, the flies were kept, as for the spiders, maybe they were crawling about in later pages. In this context, could *flies* be referring to insects in general? And what tapped on the glass were the leaves of a plant. Les mouches tissaient une toile dans les pièces ensoleillées; les mauvaises herbes qui avaient poussé près de la fenêtre frappaient méthodiquement au carreau dans la nuit. It's better with a definite article, and with the window up front, replacing glass, rather than trailing at the end.

But importantly, the image created by these sentences and some that follow, even stranger and more precise, corresponds exactly to observations made by the scientists and filmmakers, amateur or professional, who had filmed in the exclusion zone. Some species appearing where they weren't expected, photographs or shots of vegetation taking over empty rooms in abandoned houses with ruined floors and empty windows—hence the importance of the precision, of the insistence one might say, of *glass* and *window pane*, a way of saying twice that the windows had so far resisted the assaults of time and the vegetation, and that the separation of inside and outside still held. In Pripyat, what was once city, what was once forest and cultivated field can no longer be distinguished, a researcher said. You can see traces of roads and the buildings still exist because cement takes a long time to disappear, but, the researcher explained, the same plant species now grow within and outside of the city and the same animal species encounter each other in both areas.

In Dresden, where exploring the city kept me busy, where the close reading and assiduous work that every translation requires—all the more for a translation of Woolf and the pages of pure poetry that make up the middle section of *To the Lighthouse*—where the close reading and assiduous work of translation took up the majority of my time, my energy, and my mental resources, a kind of parallel life had taken shape, a life over which I had no control and which shadowed me without my knowledge. It would reveal itself at random moments, taking me by surprise and taking precedence over my actual life.

One evening, the bell of the Church of the Holy Cross, the Kreuzkirche, had just rung when I was walking along streets that had become empty. In a curve, I saw a silhouette coming toward me. I barely looked at it, I wanted to go down to the Elbe because I found the sight of the river at night calming. I wasn't thinking of anything in particular, not of anything I can remember. But I slowed my steps without even noticing, and although I couldn't distinguish the features of the person approaching me, something held me back, something familiar. As I drew close, this person became more than a silhouette, and was now a three-dimensional body I was about to pass. The figure stopped, or at least I had the sense that it did, that it was waiting for me in a way or was waiting for me to reach it. As soon as I'd noticed it, I'd had the impression that its arrival was connected to me, that it was looking for me . . . I thought of my friend who was, how should I put it, lost, gone, who was no more but was still somewhere in the world and in those who had known her. I thought of the people we pass in the street without seeing, whose image still becomes imprinted in us. I thought of all that inhabits us. I finally reached the silhouette, the unknown person, who had not moved and, although there was something strange about her—which I could not have defined—that should have frightened me, that did frighten me, I stopped, too.

Who are you? I asked.

Who do you want me to be?

Do I know you?

What do you think, was her response. It seemed to me, I believed that the words came out against my will, or rather, before I could think them up or formulate them, as if something—someone—had taken control of me to lead the conversation. A spirit, a reflex. A shade.

You're . . . on the threshold, I said hesitantly.

Don't say a name, she replied. We have no right to names.

We? Who are you? I'd have liked to ask, but these words could not overcome the obstacle, as if I didn't have the right to ask. Are you here for a while? This was not the question I wanted to ask, it made no sense.

Time does not belong to us, she said.

So then?

So then we wait.

Wait for what?

Another time.

I could say that she walked away, that she continued on her path, that she turned away, but the truth is, she was there one moment and gone the next. An erasure, an evanescence, a kind of disappearance. I was alone in the street on a moonless night. No one in the direction of the church, no one in the direction of the river, no one in the cross street that was only partly visible. I wanted only one thing, to be back in my room, where the bare, white walls looked reassuring to me because they were real. Had the scene I'd just experienced actually taken place? This shade, this figure, this silhouette, had I really seen it? Although I expected a night of insomnia, sleep suddenly bore down on me, and the next morning, there was no trace of any dreams I may have had.

When darkness fell, the stroke of the Lighthouse, which had laid itself with such authority upon the carpet in the darkness, tracing its pattern, came now in the softer light of spring mixed with moonlight gliding gently as if it laid its caress and lingered stealthily and looked and came lovingly again.

Lorsque la nuit tombait, lorsqu'il faisait sombre, lorsqu'il faisait nuit, when night fell, when it was dark, when it grew dark, le rayon du phare, qui s'était posé avec autorité sur le tapis dans le noir, traçant son dessin, venait maintenant à la lumière plus douce du printemps mêlé au clair de lune qui glissait doucement comme s'il déposait sa caresse et s'attardait furtivement, regardait et venait de nouveau avec tendresse. Staying too literal is a dead end. À la tombée de la nuit, le rayon du phare qui s'était posé avec une telle autorité sur le tapis dans le noir, dessinant sa trace, venait maintenant à la lumière plus douce du printemps, mêlé au clair de lune qui glissait doucement, comme pour poser sa caresse et s'attarder furtivement, regarder et revenir avec tendresse. Or sur le tapis dans l'obscurité. Dessinant ses motifs. Traçant son dessin . . . Drawing its patterns. Tracing its design . . .

As if applies only to *laid its caress. And lingered* picks up the course of the sentence from *came now. Came now and lingered*. The lack of a comma complicates things, makes it so that this verb can connect to this or that other one, but with rereadings, you can untangle the threads or decide on an interpretation. Which would give: À la tombée de la nuit, le rayon du phare qui se posait avec autorité sur le tapis dans l'obscurité, dessinant sa trace, venait à présent dans la lumière adoucie du printemps mêlé au clair de lune qui glissait doucement, comme pour déposer sa caresse, et s'attardait furtivement, regardait, et revenait avec tendresse.

It's a brief suspension in the change of seasons and the house's decline. The light grows softer and something like emotion appears. Mrs. Ramsay had assured her son that they could go to the lighthouse. The expedition would take place, but only later, in the third part of the novel and without Mrs. Ramsay who had passed away in an aside in the second section. And yet, Mrs. Ramsay is there: in the other characters' memories, in scenes that evoke her, in the beam of the lighthouse. The lighthouse's presence is reassuring, as was hers. And with this *caress*, with this adverb, *lovingly*, how could you not think of her? The text continues, summer follows spring once again—how many years have passed? During the *short summer nights and the long summer days*, the empty rooms seem to murmur, or rather, to vibrate with the echoes of the fields and the hum of flies. The yellow haze of sun. The rays it emits that cross the room. And Mrs. McNab, a vestige of human presence, *looked like a tropical fish oaring its way through sun-lanced waters*. Making its way as with strokes of oars. *Way* cannot be *chemin*, which is too earthbound. Everything is aquatic in this sentence or is situated between air and water. *Oaring its way*. Tel un poisson des tropiques filant à travers les eaux traversées de soleil. Filant par les eaux traversées de soleil.

I would have liked to have written, to have created a world, to have described, seen, populated it. My familiarity with the books I translate is limited to its pages. I don't see beyond what was written. Certainly, I know the text intimately, I understand it well, I can draw connections over many pages, but everything is contained in the book. I can deduce explanations, draw parallels between the author's life and what he or she had written, but it is impossible for me to retrace the process of creation, the line of thought that led someone to write a particular book. Sometimes there are letters, a diary, or different versions of the text, but all these are merely visible traces. No one has access to the creator's actual internal life. Except, perhaps, other creators.

Translation is certainly a work of recreation but it's not creation insofar as there is a foundation, a text that is not only present but also definitive, as if it had always been there, as if there had been no phases, no process, or hesitations. The only task is to stay as close as possible to the original while reproducing as best as one can its music and rhythm. I envied this friend, or rather, I admired her imaginative capacity, the way an image or a scene was transformed from something she might have recounted one day to what she put on the page, how it was both the same and different. I would leave our meetings strengthened in my desire to spend my life with books, but occasionally also a bit sad that I could not or did not know how to give shape to some of my own obsessions, which I didn't find in the books of others. Why not try it, why not write? she asked one day. I quickly replied that there already were too many people writing, my response a bit too prompt to be completely honest. Of course, I would have liked to. But hiding this desire, I said that I was too aware of the difficulty, too aware of my limitations. Trying doesn't obligate you to anything, she countered. I did try, although I didn't tell her. But I couldn't follow the thread; all I could manage were fragmentary lines that weren't even pieces of a puzzle I could assemble. I preferred not to mention it and resolved, in the future, to listen in silence the next time she suggested that I try writing.

Now and again some glass tinkled in the cupboard as if a giant voice had shrieked so loud in its agony that tumblers stood inside a cupboard vibrated too.

In French, *glass* and *tumbler* are both *verre. Tumbler* could be *gobelet*, but a goblet would sound odd in this context. One solution might be to have *verre* singular in the first case and plural in the next. The material and the object which is, after all, the idea in the text. *A giant voice.* Should I keep *the giant voice* or smooth it out with *a giant's voice*? Woolf could have written *a giant's voice* or *a gigantic voice* if she had wanted to. *A giant voice* was intentional. Why should I make it commonplace? De temps à autre le verre tintait dans les armoires comme si une voix géante hurlait si fort dans sa souffrance que des verres posés à l'intérieur d'un placard vibraient aussi. Or rather, que les verres posés à l'intérieur du placard vibraient aussi. These giant presences, without name, without contours, without form. Like the beam of the lighthouse, like the spirit that Woolf initially wanted to narrate what would become *The Waves* but disappeared over the various versions of that novel. Like the presences that vibrate around us, invisible, sometimes imperceptible and yet present. There's nothing human, as it were, in that giant voice, yet in the voice and its agony, there is something human, or at least animal. The suffering and the voice.

Then again silence fell; and then, night after night, and sometimes in plain mid-day when the roses were bright and light turned on the wall its shape clearly there seemed to drop into this silence this indifference, this integrity, the thud of something falling.

Puis le silence retomba; et puis, nuit après nuit, parfois en plein milieu du jour lorsque les roses brillaient, que la lumière projetait au mur clairement sa forme, semblait s'égoutter dans le silence, l'indifférence, l'intégrité, le bruit sourd d'une chute. *Drop*, s'égoutter—the contrast is too strong. One syllable in English, three in French. All this to avoid repeating tomber because the two English words, *fall* and *drop*, both monosyllables, have different roots. Puis de nouveau le silence tomba; et puis, nuit après nuit, parfois en plein milieu du jour lorsque les roses brillaient et que la lumière tournait vers le mur sa forme claire, semblait goutter dans le silence, l'indifférence, dans l'intégrité, le choc d'une sourde chute. Or: Puis le silence de nouveau se fit; et puis nuit après nuit, parfois en plein milieu du jour lorsque les roses brillaient et que la lumière tournait au mur sa forme claire, semblait tomber dans ce silence, cette indifférence, dans cette intégrité, le choc sourd d'une chute.

She and I talked about books, but about other things too. Life, worries, surprises—and we laughed over the anecdotes she told, or rather, the scenes I would find in her novels several years later. How can I connect or differentiate the reality described in her books and those moments of an existence, I wondered. I dealt only with the foam, with the surface, that is, with language—even if, for years, language has been raised to a divinity independent of all content. It isn't fair to speak of surface, because in faithfully translating a novel like *To the*

Lighthouse, you cannot ignore the content, the web of images and meaning, the characters that pass through it. But I liked hearing her talk about books and, back at my desk, I had the feeling that I understood more clearly what I had to do.

[*A shell exploded. Twenty or thirty young men were blown up in France, among them Andrew Ramsay, whose death, mercifully, was instantaneous.*]

Even these two sentences are not obvious. Twenty, thirty young men. For blown up, is the French word soufflés enough or do I need to qualify it with "in the explosion"? And instead of following the word order in the original, wouldn't it be better to write dont la mort fut, miséricordieusement, instantanée, whose death was, mercifully, instantaneous? And should it be un obus explosa ou une explosion d'obus, a shell exploded or the explosion of a shell? Vingt, trente jeunes hommes. No. Un obus. Vingt ou trente jeunes hommes furent soufflés dans cette explosion, parmi eux Andrew Ramsay, dont la mort fut, miséricordieusement, instantanée—I'd forgotten *in France* and because of that the rhythm is distorted if cette explosion is added. Un obus explosa. Vingt ou trente jeunes gens furent soufflés en France, au nombre desquels Andrew Ramsay, dont la mort, miséricordieusement, fut instantanée.

In two pages, Virginia Woolf dispenses with two members of the Ramsay family. Two who did not play essential roles—because it's James (the little boy who wants to go to the lighthouse), Mrs. Ramsay, and Mr. Ramsay who are the heart of the book, followed by the visitors, the entourage, the painter

Lily Briscoe, Mr. Carmichael, the one who reads Virgil, Charles Tansley the atheist, Mr. Bankes . . . Other names crop up over the course of the narrative, and, in "Time Passes," Mrs. McNab, who is watched by the objects and the vegetation.

—The convergence of times—past, present, future.

—The ecological system of the exclusion zone is similar to the one that dominated the area centuries earlier. There is talk of wolves, of Przewalski's horses, of beavers, and to a much lesser degree, of swans with yellow bills. And yet they too have reappeared, their supple and graceful outlines adding relief to the expanses of water.

—The convergence of times. The newly elected Ukrainian president decrees one July day that the forbidden zone, the exclusion zone will become a tourist area. Hiking trails will be built and cellphone coverage will be improved.

—The television series *Chernobyl* plays a part in this: its success, its fictional images replace those frequently seen pictures of a dry swimming pool or an empty classroom.

—The series plays a part, but the growth of dark tourism—catastrophe tourism—also contributes to this development. Prisons, places of genocide, massacres. To Rwanda, Auschwitz, Cambodia. To Nanjing, Korea, Hiroshima. To battlefields.

—A concept apparently created in Scotland in 1996, like its competitor, Thana- or death tourism. There is even a documentary series, *Dark Tourist,* that reports on it over eight episodes, broadcast on Netflix in 2018.

—Will the yellow-billed swan survive officially sanctioned tourism?

As for staying in Dresden—how much longer? How long can I live elsewhere, away from home? *Ailleurs,* elsewhere, probably comes from *in aliore loco*, a late Latin term, "probably" because there are other hypotheses that are rejected in the article I consulted. *Aliore* is a strange comparative of *alius*, theoretically formed by following the model of existing terms like *in interiore* or *in exteriore loco*, which would mean more or less "a more other place." An extreme otherness. And in a way, Dresden could not be more other, more elsewhere than Paris. When you leave the station, you take a large pedestrian street lined with buildings from the socialist era. In this rather unattractive area, a few original shops stand in sharp contrast to the architectural monotony of the apartment blocks and create an oasis in the concrete, in the mineral environment. Although the street occasionally has a sinister air—especially on rainy days when you have to take care not to slip—during the day it has a rather lively tenor, and nothing about it recalls the Otto Dix painting named after it, *Prague Street*—a canvas from 1920 that depicts invalids begging or moving hectically along, past frightened animals and store windows prominently displaying protheses, all in the expressionist style of the painter and his period, with grimacing, sometimes hate-filled faces and ravaged bodies in a chaotic atmosphere. Today, the windows display outdoor clothing or hiking gear instead of maimed mannequins, and pedestrians don't make their way over a kind of white mass, between cloud and hardened snow, that bodes no good, and humanity is not seen only from the perspective of a dog.

This apocalyptic scene, which I'd never seen in reality—by which I mean that I hadn't seen the original painting, which is in Stuttgart according to the Internet—had always both fascinated and frightened me with its movement, which seemed chaotic, even hysterical rather than dynamic, and prefigured the approaching fate of Germany and Prague Street. It was in Dresden that Otto Dix had studied, painted, and then taught, before being one of the first to be removed from his teaching post at the art academy. The story of his next few years was more complicated, a combination of authorizations and permits, arrest and indifference, a retreat into what was called inner emigration, then postwar honors from the two Germanies. Since looking more carefully at the details of Prague Street in the 1920 painting, I've walked along this street in the twenty-first century with a sense of gratitude for not having known it as it was before or shortly after the war, when secret inner wounds created an invisible stream flowing through the street and towns of the reconstructed country.

It was the same war that had maimed Otto Dix's caricaturized figures and, mercifully, had killed Andrew Ramsay instantaneously.

At that season those who had gone down to pace the beach and ask of the sea and sky what message they reported or what vision they affirmed had to consider among the usual token of divine bounty—

Strange, these people who paced the beach to find an answer to their questions. In the first part, some of the characters—although Woolf called the notion of characters into question—some named characters did, in fact, walk along the beach at sunset before dinner. Of them, what remains is the movement, the impulse, the need to walk by the sea. "If life has a base that it stands upon," Virginia Woolf wrote in 1939 in one of her last long texts, the autobiographical study, *A Sketch of the Past*, "if it is a bowl that one fills and fills and fills—then my bowl without a doubt stands upon this memory." The scene she then relates took place in St. Ives, in Cornwall—the landscape that inspired *To the Lighthouse*—in the nursery. The window blind must have been down because the acorn-shaped pull is drawn across the floor, but the window is open because the wind makes the shade billow. Woolf does not describe what happens but the sensations produced. With the shades down and the windows open, the memory . . . "It is of hearing the waves breaking, one, two, one, two, and sending a splash of water over the beach." The calming roar of the sea—a rhythm that accompanies an entire life.

And then there's that dash after *divine bounty*. Dashes are sometimes used the same way in English as in French, but not always. They interrupt the sentence differently. Sometimes, Virginia Woolf will use a dash to open a perspective but not close it again, so that there's only one dash. Her use of dashes was not as particular or as frequent as Marina Tsvetaeva's, who used dashes in her poems as a musical notation, indicating that some word should be thought or said in a higher or a lower tone. But in Woolf's writing—in this sentence, for example—the dash interrupts reflection, serving rather as a point of suspension, marking a pause.

—the sunset on the sea, the pallor of dawn, the moon rising, fishing boats against the moon, and children pelting each other with handfuls of grass,—something out of harmony with this jocundity, this serenity. How should I translate what is out of harmony with the jocundity, the serenity: as quelque chose ou une chose? This something appears in the next sentence.

There was the silent apparition of an ashen-coloured ship for instance, come, gone; there was a purplish stain upon the bland surface of the sea as if something had boiled and bled, invisibly, beneath. Il y avait l'apparition silencieuse d'un bateau couleur de cendre, par exemple, arrivé, reparti; il y avait une tache de pourpre sur la surface terne de la mer comme si quelque chose avait bouilli et saigné, invisible, en dessous. Arrivé, reparti—too long for *come, gone.* Il y avait l'apparition silencieuse d'un bateau couleur de cendre par exemple, venu, parti; il y avait une tache pourpre sur la surface terne de la mer comme si quelque chose avait bouilli et saigné, invisible, en dessous d'elle. Could I lighten the rhythm by moving away from the English structure? Il y avait par exemple l'apparition silencieuse d'un bateau couleur cendre, venu, reparti; une tache pourpre sur la terne surface de la mer, comme quelque chose qui aurait bouilli et saigné, invisible, en dessous.

None of these is very satisfactory—in any case, it's another allusion to the war. The boat the color of ash, the typically military gray, and the word *ashen* for the exploding shells and the resulting deaths. Then the blood. A threat, invisible but present. Everything is concentrated in these colors. That war, the First, hovered over *Jacob's Room*, over *Mrs. Dalloway*—and over Septimus Warren Smith, who could not forgive himself for having survived his friend, and could not get over having seen him die, close to him, in combat. The other war, the Second, loomed in Woolf's final novel, *Between the Acts*, in the menacing plane flying over the village. From ship to airplane, the progress of military strategy. *An ashen-coloured ship*. What concision to express the worrying strangeness of this boat on the horizon that does not resemble the familiar, innocent fishing boats in the previous sentence.

In the manuscript version, Woolf had written *murderous-looking* ship. All the work from the manuscript to the final version was one of rewriting, of erasure, not a polishing but the introduction of breaks, of metaphors, of unexpected turns of phrase. Accordingly, in the manuscript, there is a second dash in the list that enumerates the divine bounty, and this list does not differ appreciably from the final enumeration. Looking at Woolf's slightly angular handwriting, I felt as if I had forced my way into a work room, of being there, invisible, witnessing the birth of a thought, of a book. I felt I could apprehend—at the sight of the words crossed out and the handwritten additions to the first typescript—the doubt and uncertainty that might overcome the person writing these pages. And how can I explain my emotion at seeing the typewritten title, "Time Passes," and below it and in parentheses, written in Virginia Woolf's hand: (*52 Tavistock Square, London, WC 1*). Like an uncertain author sending her manuscript to an editor and adding her address for him to respond or to return the rejected work.

INTERLUDE

At night on the High Line, the spirit of the place haunts the cafés and hip stores of the Chelsea Market, recalling a past of prostitution and embracing the passage of time. The refrigerated warehouses eventually became obsolete and were abandoned. They were turned into offices, modern for their time, and these became obsolete in turn for the next generation. So runs the great cycle of architectural ecology, from one recycling to the next, occasionally with demolition pits standing by. Cranes and excavators suddenly appear, a process begins, hardhats, construction workers, the roar of motors, work continues through the night under white floodlights, and one day the metamorphosis is complete. No one remembers what stood there before, things are soon forgotten. Memory takes hold only in the provisional void, in absence, but as soon as a new presence has replaced the old, thoughts turn to required uses, consumers emerge, people who would never have turned their steps to the covered passages flanking the old delivery tracks for milk products now return constantly—the High Line has created its clientele.

Every spring, volunteers come to thin the winter growth which served as a habitat for birds needing seasonal refuge. The great spring cleaning takes a month. In rain, wind, or fine weather, the volunteer gardeners work ceaselessly, pruning, weeding, and heaping up—the discarded vegetation is ferried to Staten Island, where it will be composted and later brought downtown or elsewhere in the city to fertilize other ground. As the clippings pile up, the tracks reemerge and recall the High Line's former existence, or should we say its old identity? But the trees remain. The three-flowered maple is rare in Europe and America because it comes from China, its delicate bark peels away and drops at its foot, and in autumn, shades of red are scattered through its green foliage before crimson takes over completely. Most of the strollers walk by unaware of its rarity yet taking away a bit of its presence—maybe they will develop an interest in Chinese philosophy or a desire to see the Manchurian cranes. And that building, that solid cuboid with its eight duplex apartments designed by Japanese architect Shigeru Ban, known for his temporary edifices constructed with impermanent material to house natural-disaster refugees. Paper churches, cardboard cathedrals, emergency housing after the Kobe earthquake, after the flood of refugees into Kenya from Somalia or Sudan. But he also builds with durable material: the Seine Musicale in Boulogne-Billancourt and the apartment building visible from the High Line, the Metal Shutter Houses. He has maintained the mobile aspect of his temporary structures. Perforated metal shutters can cover the large windows completely, partially, or be raised entirely. As a result, the building's front never looks exactly the same; its outer facade can be raised or lowered, changing its entire physiognomy, while the setting sun lends its side walls a golden shimmer.

IV

A lakeshore, I said to myself, sitting in the café with the plate-glass windows opening onto the square where a Christmas market was being set up, one of the oldest in Germany, if I understood correctly. It was November, the light was growing dimmer, but there was still some brightness in the Kulturpalast and there was the movement of the tramcars. The city's hustle and bustle—as if everyone wanted to be forever on the move—was pleasant. The shores of a lake have something soothing and sad about them, an air of nostalgia, perhaps born of water's calmness, of the small waves that ripple the surface, a kind of static motion that makes you wonder what it's hiding. In the complicated geography of the ancient Underworld, wasn't the entrance often masked by a lake? Among the lakes, Avernus was one of the favorite models, a volcanic lake, deeper and more mysterious. Turner had painted it in a scene depicting Aeneus meeting the Cumaean Sybil. He made two versions about twenty years apart, which differ primarily in color, the first in rather pastel shades of yellow and orange, the second in blue hues. There is even a third, less explicit version entitled *The Golden Bough*, an additional twenty years later, which shows the lake in the background with the trees, the cliff, and the human figures taking on more prominence, and the colors becoming more muted. I vaguely remembered Aeneas's descent into the Underworld in Book 6 of the *Aeneid*. The Virgil Mr. Carmichael was reading—after all, it could have been the *Aeneid*—had Aeneas approach the Sybil's cave from the sea. I'd forgotten the rest. But in this café far from the sea and lakes, I was connected to the aquatic world thanks to the Internet, so I searched, and it didn't take long to find a website displaying the text with the Sybil's cave, her instructions on how to enter the Underworld and this evocation:

> Deep was the cave; and, downward as it went
> From the wide mouth, a rocky rough descent;
> And here th' access a gloomy grove defends,
> And there th' unnavigable lake extends,
> O'er whose unhappy waters, void of light,
> No bird presumes to steer his airy flight;
> Such deadly stenches from the depths arise,
> And steaming sulphur, that infects the skies.
>
> Tr. John Dryden

Why did I suddenly think of that particular lake, which had surprised me at the end of what seemed a long path through a forest from the train station in a small town to that lake on the outskirts of the Ravensbrück camp? I had walked through the camp, now a memorial, and the source of the unease that had dogged me through my visit—is visit the right word?— was not the long wall or the enormous statues, or the monuments and their columns, or the photographs documenting what had occurred, or the testimonies and faces of the survivors, it was, in fact, the lake so close by and so peaceful, the monstrosity of this peacefulness so near the impure exhalations of these blackish maws. Especially since, at the time, the conference on implementing the Final Solution had been held on the shore of a lake. On my way back to the train station, I had noticed the abandoned building of a supermarket—an empty cube—at the forest's edge, a few hundred meters from the camp, which had caused a scandal when it was built because of its proximity and then never opened. Strangely, the scandal arose after its construction, not before, so that it was left there, abandoned like the apartment blocks in Pripyat, evidence of a life and commerce that would never be, just as the Ferris wheel of Pripyat was evidence of festivals that would never be held—ever again.

The Elbe was so present in Dresden that I felt no immediate need for lakes, although there were many in the surrounding area. I even discovered a website that reviews lakes in Saxony, the state of which Dresden is the capital, classifying them according to a public poll, and the top lakes were those near Leipzig, Dresden's rival city. This website listed all the lakes in Germany—in the top ten, a Saxon lake, also near Leipzig, was fourth. And I, I drifted, on the edge of lakes, far from lakes. One day that same summer, the philosopher Ágnes Heller, who spent her vacations on Lake Balaton, swam out and did not return. That is what the announcement said. In the various languages I know, it was expressed the same way. She went swimming and did not return. Did not return. You could imagine her reaching the other shore to disappear and start a new life—but the lake is twelve kilometers wide, and she had just celebrated her ninetieth birthday. Then, a body was found and identified as hers. So the alternatives were exhaustion, illness—but the autopsy revealed no trace—or a conscious choice. Of course, the circumstances of her death were insignificant compared to her writing, her lectures, her struggle against dictatorship, but they completed the image of a life dedicated to freedom and it was difficult not to think that she had exercised this liberty to the final moment.

—Before *The Edge of the World*, Michael Powell had made several films—juvenilia, as they say. Particularly *The Phantom Light* in 1935.

—The film opens with the image of a train. Alone in a compartment, a man is looking at a piece of paper on which is written "Chief Lightkeeper." The train arrives in Wales.

—*The Edge of the World* also opens with an arrival, this one by sea.

—Here we are inland. You can only reach the sea after a long journey.

—The lighthouse is haunted, they say, a scene of mysterious deaths. At night, the lighthouse's beacon goes out. A phantom light flickers on the rocks on which deep-sea vessels are wrecked.

—A lighthouse in the open sea, glorious views of rough, swirling waters, of the lens—the eye that surveys. The light flashes in the night, the ship pitches, shaken by the waves.

—The movie was filmed in a lighthouse off the coast of Wales, using all its resources, the vertiginous height of the sheer cliff face from the moving surface of the sea, the imposing mechanism, the interior staircases and the external railing, the different levels, the rigging, the walls and smooth cliff faces.

—The night, the sea—and the beam of the lighthouse.

The work I was doing in Dresden I could have done in Paris because, after all, did I really need to be somewhere else if I was spending hours in front of my computer examining the beauties of "Time Passes"? But what had pushed me to leave was still inside me and was inducing me to delay my inevitable return past the end of my fellowship. I carried within me the dreams and obsessions, the awakenings, the visions. In the café which I had made my favorite spot, there were regulars I was getting to know, or rather, recognize, and they began to recognize me. One of them came up to me not long ago to ask if I was writing. No, I said, I'm translating.

That dream, then, of sharing, completing, finding in solitude on the beach an answer, was but a reflection in a mirror, and the mirror itself was but the surface glassiness which forms in quiescence when the nobler powers sleep beneath?

The words are relatively simple here, but the sentence is not. Et ce rêve de partage, d'achèvement, de réponse trouvée sur la plage dans la solitude ne serait qu'un reflet dans un miroir, et le miroir lui-même que la surface vitrifiée qui se forme dans le calme lorsque les puissances plus nobles en dessous sont endormies? Et le miroir lui-même, la surface vitrifiée qui se forme calmement quand de nobles puissances, au-dessous, or rather, quand les nobles puissances, au-dessous, sont endormies? I try, but each time something disrupts, obstructs the fluidity of the whole. And that majestic word, *quiescence*, while rare, cannot be rendered with the banality of *calme. Calmement* is a bit better because longer. But it's also imperfect. I'll have to resign myself to continuing without really having found a solution.

Impatient, despairing yet loth to go (for beauty offers her lures, has her consolations), to pace the beach was impossible; contemplation was unendurable; the mirror was broken.

For beauty offers her lures? . . . presents her lures? What the text, the novel, the author seems to say is that the answer can no longer be found in the soothing power of nature. It no longer has consolations. Had it ever? Isn't it illusory to think you can find answers by pacing the beach? And could I believe that I wouldn't find in Dresden what I was escaping in Paris? Besides, wasn't I convinced that I saw, didn't I actually see a silhouette in the street at night? I had been taking detours since that night, I wanted to avoid that street—pretending to believe or actually believing that the silhouette was part of the street and not my life.

[*Mr. Carmichael brought out a volume of poems that spring, which had an unexpected success. The war, people said, has revived their interest in poetry.*]

Is this ironically meant? It's true that a generation of poets arose during the First World War. They were called the *war poets*, but this was also because many of them, like Siegfried

Sassoon, Rupert Brooke, and Wilfred Owen, had died in this war. Woolf had met Rupert Brooke when she was still Virginia Stephen. They had played together as children in St. Ives, in Cornwall, and had continued to meet. In a letter dated April 8, 1925, Virginia Woolf wrote that "in fact, Bloomsbury was against [Brooke] and he against them." She went on to write that she hadn't thought he would be a poet. She thought that he, an ambitious man, would have a political career and edit the classics in his spare time. His poems of the time were "all adjectives and contortions." She must read them again, she concluded. Did she? It seems doubtful. Nor does she mention in her letters or diary the night when Rupert Brooke apparently suggested they swim naked in a pond.

I rarely went out at night from then on, and not because of the cold, the dampness, the night. Sometimes I would cross the Elbe, thinking for some reason that nothing would pursue me there, perhaps because the city, despite the majesty of the buildings on the riverbank, seemed to live more in the present with its lively streets and cafés, the young people, its alternative places, and I dove into the delights of discovery and of forgetting. But on the way back, on the bridge, when I saw the towers and domes looming in the darkness, the skyline to which Dresden owed and still owes its fame, I was filled with anxiety until I reached my room, whose spareness seemed to chase away the phantoms.

In that room one night, I came across Michael Powell's film on YouTube: *The Phantom Light*, full of staircases and doors, windows, faces that were difficult to identify in the dark, moving lanterns, fog, bells, chaotic movement. A lighthouse, eight years after Virginia Woolf's. The most extraordinary sequence came one hour and nine minutes into the movie, almost four minutes before the end, at the moment the lighthouse is relit, the camera shows only the Fresnel lens, the faces, the ship about to crash against the rocks, then again the lens, the light returning, the waves, the compass showing the ship's abrupt course correction, the waves, its wake in the water, the lens, the mechanism, the absolute darkness, the lens, and then, after these constant cuts of no more than thirty seconds, the calm returns—the ship is back on course. Naturally, this lighthouse was much more fanciful, adventurous, and much less existential or metaphysical than Woolf's, but I saw in it a sign, having found the movie by chance, on a random search for which I hadn't entered the word lighthouse in French or English—a sign that translating this work at this moment in my life had meaning.

In Woolf's preparatory notes for *To the Lighthouse*, there is a drawing of a kind of H, two vertical spaces joined by a horizontal one. In March 1925, *Mrs. Dalloway* had just appeared. *Two blocks joined by a corridor.* "Time Passes" is this corridor. Time passes through a simple corridor. Like the brackets added later, which contain events that might have been thought essential and that in traditional novels constitute the main action—marriage, war, death. This corridor, although necessarily narrower than the two blocks it joins, isn't it the heart of the novel that Woolf liked to call an elegy? The brackets isolate what they contain. But do they set off the contents to make it an element that belongs to a second zone, or do they set it off because, isolated from the rest, the contents have a particular status? Woolf wrote once, I no longer know where, that the brackets allow her to draw attention to multiple events occurring simultaneously.

One evening, as I was following my now-familiar route later than usual, I looked down from the bridge at the river's black water whose sluggish current has a soothing effect and thought I felt a light touch, a presence, an imperceptible change in the atmosphere, and then it was gone. Perhaps the wind had picked up; there was no one around. Then the sensation returned after a short distance, and I picked up my pace. I heard a kind of voice murmuring indistinctly. The voice was clear, or rather, I was sure that I'd heard it and that it didn't come from my thoughts.

This shape before me, was it she? Was there a form? No passersby, not a single car, as if everything had stopped—the city of Dresden was suspended between past and present. And the Elbe? I couldn't make anything out in the dark, not even the current that would have reassured me, the river's ceaseless movement from its source to the sea. I looked upstream, but the water was as mysteriously motionless as it was downstream. Even the clouds weren't moving. The sky was uniformly overcast, without stars. As for the moon, where was it? There was no way to avoid the encounter. If anyone had passed, anyone at all, I would have rushed toward him and asked him to accompany me to my lodging. To "lodge," I'd never appreciated as much the full meaning of the word, including protection from the unpredictability of the elements. But there was no one I could ask. I would have to make it alone to that seemingly unreachable harbor. There was half of the bridge left to cross, and even though the building with the tall door was near the river, I'd still have to cover a few meters, pass a street that was often empty even by day, walk around a group of apartment blocks before reaching the street where I lived—where I was lodging temporarily.

What are you doing here? Is it really you?

I didn't know if I was speaking out loud. I could no longer distinguish between word and thought. An unusual connection had formed, a connection beyond words, or rather, beyond their sound. It was enough to think the words for them to speed toward their destination—but that was still too precise a designation for an imperceptible, elusive process.

Me? she said. I no longer know who that is.

But are you here because of me?

I don't understand. We are indistinguishable.

We? Who's that?

Us, I don't know anything else.

Do you live there?

Live doesn't mean anything. We float, we walk.

Wander? I ask.

I don't know, she replied. I'm looking for the sea. Do you know where it is?

I pointed in the other direction, away from Dresden and its environs, toward the north and Hamburg, and on to the

North Sea. She disappeared. I looked toward the distant sea, hoping to see a shape, even if faint, but I saw nothing and her disappearance left me with a mixture of relief and regret.

—It's a journey, a circle drawn in Europe across the seas. Brussels, then Guernsey, then back to Brussels—before returning to Paris.

—Like *Les Misérables*, like *Toilers of the Sea*, *The Man Who Laughs* is a novel Hugo wrote in exile—the last in such circumstances. Almost Hugo's final novel. After it, there will only be *Ninety-Three*.

—"Most of this book," Hugo wrote, "was written on Guernsey, but it was begun in Brussels on July 21, 1866 and finished in Brussels on August 23, 1868." *The Man Who Laughs* was published the following year to little success. "Is it I who am mistaken? Is it my time?" Hugo asked. His doubts did not last long. In the following sentence, he replied, "If I believed I were mistaken, I would remain silent."

—In the eleventh chapter of the second part, entitled "The Caskets," there's the description of a lighthouse that matches the Eddystone Lighthouse in Cornwall, but closer to Devon than St. Ives. A lighthouse Hugo had drawn as well as described.

—"In the nineteenth century, a lighthouse is a tall conoid cylinder of masonry, topped with a completely scientific machinery for casting light." "In the seventeenth century, a lighthouse was a kind of tuft planted on land at the coast. The architecture of lighthouses was magnificent and extravagant."

—Hugo quotes the Eddystone Lighthouse's motto—*Pax in bello*—and adds "this declaration of peace did not always disarm the ocean," before evoking Henry Winstanley's first construction of the lighthouse at his own expense on a wild spot near Plymouth. "When the tower was finished, he shut himself inside it and had it tested by the storm."

—There would be two more versions of the lighthouse before the current one, designed by James Douglass and inaugurated in 1882—the year Virginia Woolf was born.

Night after night, summer and winter, the torment of storms, the arrow-like stillness of fine weather, held their court without interference.

Nuit après nuit, été et hiver, le tourment des tempêtes, l'immobilité de flèche du beau temps, donnaient leur spectacle sans interférence. Night after night, in summer as in winter, the torment of storms, the immobility of fine weather's arrow presided in their pageantries without interference. . . . se donnaient en spectacle sans interférence. . . . offered their pageantry without interference. Nuit après nuit, été comme hiver, le tourment des tempêtes, la flèche immobile du beau temps donnaient leur spectacle sans interférence. Night after night, in summer as in winter, the torment of storms, fine weather's immobile arrow presented their pageant without interference. Nuit après nuit, été ou hiver, le tourment des tempêtes, l'immobile flèche du beau temps donnaient leur spectacle sans interférence. Night after night, in summer or winter, the torment of storms, the immobile arrow of fine weather held their court without interference.

So many hesitations and approximations. The approach is gradual, made by stages, like a landing, a slow descent. Sometimes we re-ascend—in a reworked version that is worse than the previous one—then we return to the lower altitude and keep descending until the moment of relief when the wheels finally touch ground. The image isn't perfect, of course. It depends, after all, on how you look at it. It's not that the translation is above the original, although it hovers; at first it floats, untethered, then gradually nears its foundation, the rendition of the text is in sight, it takes on contours, more precise forms emerge, and the moment arrives when it rests on a solid base, on firm ground.

Without interference means that no human presence—no artificial light—troubles the succession of nights or distinguishes summer from winter. Was there a depiction in literature before this of a landscape, a climate, a house without inhabitants? There's no need for explication—or, from this point of view, for the few preceding sentences in brackets that spin a slender thread of human time—"Time Passes" evokes the first forbidden zone, the first desolation, and it makes little difference if the cause is unknown; in this uninhabited universe, everything is coherent, it is all consistent, logic holds, nothing changed except that there was no interference—as there would be no interference several decades later somewhere in Ukraine. This, in turn, reveals the euphemism of current slogans that, intending to raise our awareness, proclaim the planet is threatened, whereas the planet is not in danger—the human race is.

I was in Dresden. Suddenly, my logic finally seemed logical. Here I was in a city once destroyed by aerial bombing, translating a text that speaks, in its own fashion, of time's destruction and the destruction of time by man, of the disappearance of a house's inhabitants representing a greater disappearance, a more comprehensive absence. I had surely mentioned this in my application for the residency grant, but as an abstract thought. Now I was living this thought. I looked at the houses, the buildings, which had seemed until then to be nothing more than the simple backdrop of my roaming—except for a few specific locations, like the café in the Kulturpalast—as if they were discrete beings, newcomers or survivors, depending on whether they dated from before or after that night of February 1945, the memory of which, commemorated every year, continued to haunt the city. City of hauntings. The haunting of the past and that of the future with those populist groups that assembled, week after week, on a square turned into an entrenched encampment, a refuge for those who wanted time to stand still like an arrow . . . Woolf's *arrow-like stillness* is paradoxical, but I understood it as an allusion to Zeno's paradox, that of Achilles and the tortoise; if we divide a span of time into moments, in each moment the arrow is immobile even if it is in motion; similarly, Achilles will never catch up to the tortoise that has had a head start—even if he does, in fact, catch up to it.

From that point on, newly attentive to the city, I divided my time between immobility (in my room or the Kulturpalast café) and walks on which I traced expanding circles—in search of a meaning, an explanation, a presence. In the streets by day or night, I expected at every moment to see, to meet again the shape that had followed me or passed me, the one I'd spoken with and that seemed to have completely vanished. Someone who did not resemble my friend but recalled her. A correspondence between my memories and my thoughts. The materialization of this correspondence, of this mental overlap. So does she not exist? Is she merely an emanation from my call, from my need to find something that had not been completely extinguished? Some remainder of a body or mind? But why did no one appear in the past few days when I had been thinking no more or less often of her than when she had come? Should I return to the bridge? Could I only see and talk to her in interstices—between two shores, two worlds, between past and present?

After a description of the tumbling and tossing battle of the winds, the furious nocturnal universe, the leviathan waves lunging and plunging in the darkness, of all the sounds that could be heard from the rooms of the empty house, the spring garden emerges, unaltered.

Violets came and daffodils. But the stillness and the brightness of the day were as strange as the chaos and tumult of the night, with the trees standing there, and the flowers standing there, looking before them, looking up, yet beholding nothing, eyeless, and so terrible.

Who is looking? The trees? The flowers? The stillness and brightness of the day? The present participle does not give any indication of number. Singular or plural, it's the same. What to do? Reread the sentence.

But the stillness and the brightness of the day were as strange as the chaos and tumult of the night, with the trees standing there, and the flowers standing there, looking before them, looking up, yet beholding nothing, eyeless, and so terrible.

The repeated *-ing* sound. A strict rhythm. Mais la tranquillité et la clarté du jour étaient aussi étranges que le chaos et le tumulte de la nuit, avec les arbres qui étaient là, avec les fleurs qui étaient là, regardant au-devant, regardant en l'air, et pourtant n'apercevant rien, puisque sans yeux et si terribles. Not so bad but it has that *puisque*—because eyeless—an explanation that is not in Woolf's text, in which *eyeless* stands alone, concise, sufficient in itself, containing its own explanation—but in French? Can you say et pourtant n'apercevant rien, sans yeux et terribles? sans yeux et si terribles. Et pourtant n'apercevant rien, sans yeux, et terribles. It seems to me that adding *puisque*, for because without eyes, is a lesser evil.

This apparent order, more terrible than chaos, isn't it the same one as in the exclusion zone around Chernobyl where nature has returned with abundant species, a peaceful lushness with the trees standing there, and the flowers standing there, looking before them, seeing nothing . . . Nature has returned but differently, strangely disquieting, too present. Trees that would have been cut down because they were diseased still stood, and their presence has had one effect on the forest while their absence would have had a different one. A nature fully present surrounds Chernobyl without absence, or rather, it's a world in which nothing disappears. Everything remains or is transformed in the slow time of decomposition. The phantoms remain.

INTERLUDE

On the High Line, everything is calculated, everything has a meaning. You walk on loosely joined planks without thinking about them while other planks have a regular design, and still others have thin slits cut into them to let the vegetation intrude amid the concrete, and like the wild grasses farther off, the ferns and random flowers create an impression of untamed nature taking over the city, or rather, of nature that knows how to live in harmony with the city, or rather, of a city that knows how to live in harmony with nature. But these concrete slabs come one after the other as regularly as railway ties. The planks of the benches that punctuate the walkway also recall rails and ties. Everything touches on the past and points to the future. The High Line is a book we leaf through hastily, skimming it from one end to the other, or linger over, descending again to the arteries of city traffic, then climbing back up a flight of stairs, a book we can read, interrupting our reading now and then, stopping on a bench to look at the ephemeral installations that occasionally adorn it or enjoying the view of the piers or the cranes towering over constructions sites.

The first three decades of the twentieth century were the moment of glory for the Chelsea piers inaugurated in 1910. Ocean liners departed from these piers, including, one summer day in 1936, the SS *Manhattan*, which carried American athletes, among them Jessie Owens, to the Olympic Games in Berlin.

An imposing grayish-brown building stands on the corner of 11th Avenue and West 20th Street. As a Seaman's House YMCA, it offered accommodation to merchant sailors while their ships were docked at the Chelsea piers. It also provided shelter from the cold, the wind, and the dangers of the night. But with the decline of maritime commerce, there were fewer and fewer sailors. The building was converted into a drug-treatment center, then into a women's prison. On the roof, an open-air structure enclosed with metal fencing served as a terrace from which the prisoners could catch glimpses of urban life and a stretch of sky and horizon and hear the bustle of the city. But the prison was evacuated because of Hurricane Sandy in 2012. At the urging of community organizers and women's rights advocates, the building was slated to be transformed into a Women's Building, but now is likely to be converted into affordable housing units and supportive housing for the formerly homeless. Following current tendencies in architecture and urban planning—to redo rather than undo, to conserve through transformation—the building's interior configuration will not be destroyed. You could call it a kind of ecological philosophy, recycling, transformism. Recognizing the past beneath the layer of the present. Still, most often we know nothing of a site's history, and we pass buildings that remain silent about their future fates and their former inhabitants.

West 20th Street was once a boundary between two parts of the High Line, dividing it into a north and a south section, a division previously marked with a metal grille that was removed several years ago. Is the atmosphere really any different north of West 20th? Are the landscaping, the vegetation, and the flora subject to a different climate? The walkway seems narrower, lined as it is with taller buildings, and the sky seems more elusive. However, if you walk along the High Line with no interest in its past, it's unlikely that you will notice a change. But maybe you'll retain a memory of this area, which one enters like a secret forest, even if the impression doesn't last, even if you were caught up in a conversation; maybe you'll have noticed a change in the light, a shadow that passes and turns your thoughts in another direction.

V

The scene was a large bay at night with two lights, one red and the other white, flashing alternately in the distance, like two signals sent to observers. Don't worry, they said, we're here to watch over you, the ocean, and the world. They were visible from land and sea. They had a double meaning, a double function: to reassure the navigators and sailors, and to reassure those walking on the beach. The beam was to reassure those who were looking for a passage, a course, but its calming presence—too distant for it to be more than an intermittent presence—also had an unsettling aspect, perhaps the uncertainty of a mirage, of an illusion, for in those seconds during which nothing existed but the night's profound darkness, who could be certain that the brief brightness would return? Despite the distance—how many dozens of kilometers—something urged one to pause, far away and yet through this call bound to the night, the ocean, and the cosmos. There was a sense of something escaping to rejoin the universe. The image remained and with it the feeling, the emotion imprinted in our innermost being and become a part of it and serving as a shield against life's disappointments—answers ungiven, things undone, people who don't understand.

The ancient, the modern—this eternal dispute runs through every era and every field. It resurfaces in *The Edge of the World*. But first we see . . . stone houses, boarded up window frames, a *Post Office* sign (the letters are barely legible), an empty landscape. Superimposed on these are people. Almost transparent silhouettes. We see the shapes and the movement, those who are leaving like so many before them and so many after them. The slow movement of those walking, those leaving. Later in the film is a procession, a church, people dressed in black, the tolling of bells. The old and the new. One villager—Robbie—wants to leave, the other—Andrew—to stay. To remain on the island and live like before. And since the community cannot choose between the two, a fight will decide the matter. Not a duel with swords but the scaling of a cliff at its steepest point. In the traditional way, barehanded and without ropes. If Andrew reaches the top first, or Robbie does, that will decide whether the island will be inhabited or deserted. But things don't turn out as planned. Robbie loses his grip. Andrew rushes to save him—too late. Robbie is the brother of Ruth who is Andrew's fiancée. Peter Mason is Robbie and Ruth's father, it is his name that is carved into the stone with the words *gone over*.

Cities are made of their buildings and their inhabitants, that is, of solid, unmoving presences and mobile presences—voices, shadows, traces. Something of us, someone who resembles someone we know or resembles a thought that occurs to us while something like a perfume, a whisper, a name wafts along the street. From one avenue to another, our thoughts form a stream of parallel traffic, invisible but as significant as—if not more so than—the visible stream of traffic. Silent. Invincible.

It was yesterday. I wasn't taking a stroll—at that point in Dresden, I only went for walks in new neighborhoods, exploring parts of the city I didn't know. There are many of these areas on both sides of the Elbe. The city offers itself up to the gaze at the same time as it closes in on its secrets, its wounds, its glorious history followed by the night of the bombing, the years of being closed off and the years of rejecting outsiders. It was yesterday. I wasn't taking a stroll, I was walking on the other side of the river, passing through a maze of back courtyards and narrow streets buzzing with the voices of students who gathered in the evenings, prolonging their day past its final hours just as I wanted to prolong mine, but alone and unknown to all. I walked until I was very tired, to be sure that I would fall asleep in my monastic room, without thinking, without any of the words from the work I was translating—that I was trying to translate—running through my mind, without any lighthouse beam interrupting my nights. And then I saw something, someone. When I reached the broad avenue that leads to the bridge, I noticed a figure on the other side, the same one, again. She was coming closer, it seemed, or I was the one approaching her. She appeared to be waiting for me, yes, that was it, she was waiting for me. I tried not to pick up my pace, tried to act as if everything was normal, as if the moment after resembled the moment before. But my attempts were in vain and the thoughts that had been interrupted did not return, instead they left behind a void as preparation for what was to come.

The sea, she said.

(I write *she* but it was a nameless shape, even if it resembled the friend who did have a name.)

I showed you the direction.

(It felt strange to speak so informally, but it would have felt just as strange to address her politely. Perhaps I should have avoided *tu* or *vous* and used other words—or thoughts.)

I followed the river. I didn't get to the sea.

Maybe you stopped too soon. Maybe the sea was farther on.

I saw a port.

And then?

(The conversation was almost reassuring, mundane, with simple topographical facts. Around us—an *us* that made me shiver—the city's night, its muted lights, the sensation of water flowing nearby, of the port, of hovering spires and domes.)

I turned back.

Too soon.

When I wanted to.

And then?

I'd forgotten.

You forgot something?

Something to say.

That you wanted to say to someone?

Maybe.

(I tried to keep the tone neutral, to emphasize the materiality of words rather than their indifference, to keep to the referential side of language—as they say—in describing the external world, communicating information, staying factual. To keep from thinking, for example, that this person could be me.)

And what was it you wanted to say?

The moment has passed.

I couldn't have said with confidence that we were speaking aloud, that we were speaking, nor could I have called it a kind of transmission of thought to thought. Even today, I only know that there was a shape, there was something, someone before me and then suddenly there was nothing. An absence. It wasn't that the shape had dissolved. There was no transition between presence and absence. It wasn't even absence—because in absence there's still a trace of presence—but a void. As if there'd never been anything.

The house remained empty and was surely going to be sold. Mrs. McNab picked a bunch of flowers in the garden because it would have been a pity to let them waste.

There it had stood all these years without a soul in it.

Elle était restée toutes ces années sans une âme à l'intérieur. Elle était restée là, durant toutes ces années, sans âme qui vive. It had stood there, all these years, without a living soul. Do I need to add à l'intérieur for *in it*? And âme qui vive, living soul, or without a person in it? Although in English you say *soul*, in French you'd say person. It, elle—the house, la maison. Stood there, necessarily *without a soul in it*. In the preceding passages, the house was described as living through the life of objects and the wind, following the rhythm of the seasons and the elements. Mrs. McNab is the first human presence in a long time. But the house was too large a burden, cleaning it all too much work; it was beyond her strength. *She was too old. Her legs pained her.*

All those books needed to be laid out on the grass in the sun; there was plaster fallen in the hall; the rain pipe had blocked over the study window and let the water in; the carpet was ruined quite.

Tous ces livres devaient être déposés dans l'herbe au soleil; du plâtre était tombé dans l'entrée; la gouttière au-dessus de la fenêtre du bureau s'était bloquée et laissait entrer l'eau; le tapis était presque entièrement ruiné. All those books had to be spread out on the grass in the sun; some plaster had fallen in the hall; the rain pipe had become blocked over the study window and let the water in; the carpet was almost completely ruined. Tous ces livres, il fallait les déposer sur l'herbe au soleil; il y avait du plâtre tombé dans le hall; la gouttière était bouchée au niveau de la fenêtre du bureau et l'eau pénétrait; le tapis était quasiment ruiné. All those books would have to be put out on the grass in the sun; plaster had fallen in the hall; the rain pipe was blocked at the height of the study window and water was coming in; the carpet was almost ruined. Au niveau de la fenêtre du bureau, at the height of the study window—how awkward.

These are the first major damages inside the house. The drafts blowing through it, the few flowers picked because no one came. Life seems to have taken hold of the objects, all this was nothing compared to the damage that would come with time. Already one of the elements—water—had erased the borders, overflowed the boundaries.

But people should come themselves; they should have sent somebody down to see.

Down to see. London is north of Cornwall. But the novel—the elegy—is set on the Isle of Skye, north of London. *Sent somebody down*—did the word just slip out for Woolf, her idea of an actual location briefly overshadowing the imagined one? Or was it just a way of saying *they should have sent somebody to see*, as common as the other with a syllable added for a more satisfying rhythm?

For there were clothes in the cupboards; they had left clothes in all the bedrooms. What was she to do with them? They had the moth in them—Mrs. Ramsay's things.

They had moths in them—Mrs. Ramsay's things. Or rather, they were full of moths—Mrs. Ramsay's things. Or, there were moths inside—of Mrs. Ramsay's things. *Moth*—the word signifies both the larger Lepidoptera and the clothes moth whose larvae eat fabrics. *Moth* is generally translated into French as *phalène*, and clothing moth as *mite*. In the original manuscript in the Berg Collection, even though this passage differs only slightly from the final text, the moth is not in Mrs. Ramsay's clothing. And yet, this moth will haunt Woolf's oeuvre. On May 3, 1927, Virginia Woolf receives a letter from her sister, Vanessa Bell, who is in the south of France, in Cassis. She writes about trying to catch moths for her children, the way the two of them had liked collecting butterflies. One night, a moth banged against the window so loud, everyone thought someone had knocked on the door. Virginia Woolf answers her on May 8: "By the way, your story of the Moth so fascinates me that I am going to write a story about it. I could think of nothing else but you and the moths for hours after reading your letter."

The moth is the source of *The Waves,* which was first titled *The Moths*. Is it the memory of this letter that ripples through the pages of another work that describes the death of a moth, or rather, describes a harmless September morning on which a similar energy animates the birds, the horses, and the moth fluttering at the window? But the moth grew stiff and then its movements became frantic. The observer suddenly realizes that its death was approaching. What beauty, what emotion there is in the contrast between the tiny legs and the enormous doom that awaits—what power there is in Woolf's description of the moth's agitation as a desperate protest against death. The story was published in a posthumous volume in 1942, but when had it been written? Can we suppose that having left *The Moths* when it became *The Waves*, the moths had flown to other texts and that one of them had landed in the corner of a window while the writer was lost in thought, or perhaps thinking of nothing, and her eyes were drawn to that vain struggle, whose import she gradually came to understand?

Mrs. Ramsay's things . . .

There were boots and shoes; and a brush and comb left on the dressing table, for all the world as if she expected to come back tomorrow.

Il y avait des bottes et des chaussures; et une brosse et un peigne sur la coiffeuse, exactement comme si elle pensait être de retour le lendemain. Comme si elle pensait revenir le lendemain. Il y avait des chaussures et des bottes (sentences sounds better in French when you put the longer word before the shorter one—des chaussures et des bottes rather than des bottes et des chaussures). Il y avait des chaussures et des bottes; une brosse et un peigne laissés sur la coiffeuse, exactement comme si elle pensait revenir le lendemain.

Like in that abandoned classroom in Pripyat, the tables and chalkboard, the chairs, toys, and open books—images that spread around the world on the Internet and in other media, that spread through minds and have turned Pripyat into the symbol of an interrupted world, a world that no longer holds.

—Sunrise.

—A city in Florida of almost 90,000 people.

—As in every city, there are streets, cinemas, schools, shops, police, cars to buy or rent, an IKEA store, sports teams, everything you need. No different from other cities.

—But in September 2010, Sunrise disappeared from Google Maps for a whole month.

—It's not very serious, people thought, because the physical city still exits.

—Well, no, actually, the city no longer existed. If you were looking for a locksmith, an electrician, a plumber, if you wanted a repairman, a café, a dentist, someone or something in Sunrise, you wouldn't find anything, not an address, a name, or a telephone.

—One day we woke up and no longer existed, the mayor said.

—Please accept our apologies, Google said, it's a bug, a technical error.

—Sunrise exists again. The sun rises anew.

Life on Foula/Hirta goes on as before—not entirely, that is, because Robbie's father cannot bear Andrew's presence and withdraws in silent reproach. Ironically, Andrew, who wanted the island to remain inhabited, has to leave for the mainland to escape the silence. Ruth is pregnant and events follow quickly. The baby is born, is ill, everything possible is done to transport the infant to the mainland. Andrew is the one who comes to get the mother and child. The meaning of the overlapping shadows at the beginning becomes clear: it's the entire population leaving the island—all but Peter, who scales the cliff his son had climbed. The rope frays. Peter falls.

Gone over.

I never expected that I would come to care for this city, that I'd go so far as to like that charmless *Prager Strasse*, Prague Street, the large pedestrian artery lined with shops that have retained their former structure, the large, rectangular shop windows behind which, from East Germany to the Soviet Union, were bookstores or children's shops or Gastronom shops that sold a selection of food products, the stock entirely dependent on what was delivered. These shops were succeeded by chain stores, sometimes by luxury brands, but the street retained something of the past, maybe in its proportions or in the number of elderly people one saw who had known the previous regime or in the apartment buildings that lined it. Did it have something to do with being far away or from elsewhere, with having the lightness of people who have no history? Even if I carried emptiness and absence inside me? Was it the company of Woolf's text that seemed to me to contain, in its way, the entirety of the world? Did I need to find a reason? Dresden opened itself up to me without reservation. I looked at the few murals that survived socialism on this or that side street or on the more visible facade of the restored Kulturpalast. Would I stay after finishing my translation? The questions brushed against me constantly. I surrendered completely to the moment and lived on an island of time and on the island of the novel, in the abandoned house in which someone, Mrs. McNab, despite her weakness, her pains, and her age, tried to keep some order in the chaos.

She was dead, they said; years ago, in London.

In one sentence, we have the confirmation of the earlier brackets. In one sentence, time passes. In the brackets, Mrs. Ramsay's death happened suddenly at night. Now it's years later. In London. How far away the large city seems in this environment, almost fragile . . . And now her clothes are abandoned to their fate just as the garden was abandoned to the rabbits digging in the earth. Once again, in parentheses:

(*She had died very sudden at the end, they said.*)

Elle était morte très soudainement à la fin, disaient-ils. Morte à la fin, doesn't work. Elle avait eu une fin très soudaine, disaient-ils. Her end was very sudden they said. Here her death disappears behind the end, but how else can I translate it? Finalement, elle avait eu une mort soudaine, disaient-ils. In the end, she had died very suddenly, they said. Maybe . . .

I told her that when I receive a work to translate, I feel like I'm seeing a charging wild animal. It frightens me; the entire difficulty lies in taming it. I need to read the new text right away; I put everything else aside to reassure myself, to confirm that, for all its challenges and serious obstacles, I can manage it. Then the wild animal becomes less threatening; I just have to feed it according to its expectations, to talk and listen to it. This made her laugh. And despite my experience—until now, each wild animal has allowed itself to be tamed—the fear remains. Each new arrival brings with it the risk that the wild animal will devour me, and the fear only dissipates after I've read the whole text.

What about writing a novel? No, she said, it's not like that. It's a patient construction, without the ferocity, without the fear of devastation I described. The fear—for there was fear—was of silence, of absence, of trails leading nowhere, or of a mass of banalities, of which you're initially unaware, which you may even consider real finds until a second reading reveals them to be what they are: sentences to cross out. I'd have liked to tell her that when I'm translating "Time Passes," I sometimes consult the first draft and there, too, lines are crossed out, there are sentences that don't appear in the next version, phrases that float up to the surfaces like flotsam from a shipwreck. Woolf also hesitated, I'd have liked to say to my writer friend, she wrote what she wouldn't have wanted to write and realizes only later, but this was my first translation that I couldn't discuss with her. It was the first time I had to make this journey without her.

And once they had been coming, but had put off coming, what with the war, and travel being so difficult these days;

Et une fois ils devaient venir mais avaient remis leur visite, en raison de la guerre, des voyages difficiles à entreprendre en ces temps . . . And once they were meant to come, but had put off their visit because of the war, and travel being so difficult these days. Each attempt to render the soberness of the English text using words that are indistinguishable from an everyday vocabulary meets impossible hurdles in French. Une fois ils avaient failli venir mais avaient renoncé, à cause de la guerre . . . Once they'd been meaning to come would be closer despite the changes to the sentence. Let's leave it there for now and keep going. The main thing is to create a rough version that will serve as a foundation for revision, which promises to be a long process.

they had never come all these years; just sent her money;

Ils n'étaient jamais venus, toutes ces années; lui avaient juste envoyé de l'argent.

Four words in English, seven in French. Four short words—and that "just," an unsatisfying Anglicism. Should I leave it out? Ils n'étaient jamais venus, durant toutes ces années; lui avaient envoyé de l'argent. I'm not sure. . . . s'étaient contenté de lui envoyer de l'argent. They'd been content to send her money. Closer in meaning but too long, much too long.

but never wrote, never came, and expected to find things as they had left them, ah dear!

Mais sans écrire, sans venir, et s'attendant à tout retrouver, mon Dieu, comme ils l'avaient laissé! But without having written, without having come, and expecting to find things as they had left them, my goodness! Or in the past perfect? But hadn't written, hadn't come, oh dear, and expected to find things as they had left them!

Mrs. Ramsay's image floated in Mrs. McNab's memory, briefly revived as it would be revived in her children's memory in the next section, a measure of the difference between the times before and those after, a symbol of the true meaning of the word "nevermore."

Nevermore, I said to myself, would we have our regular meetings in a spot whose name never changed, although the owner often did. On a corner in the quartier des Halles in Paris, in the center of the city—a very different city from the one I was in now, a city that had not been destroyed except by certain development projects that had, no doubt, retained too much from previous eras to be truly renewed, to be of their time. Chinese cuisine reinterpreted, Moroccan food with a décor to match, then another renovation and a relegation to a mediocre pizzeria—over the years, the staff changed, the taste changed, the furniture changed, as did the décor. But loyal to the name, we kept meeting there because it was convenient to meet in the same place without having to look for somewhere new. And we met at the same time as well, so that all we had to do was decide on a date to talk about our work and our lives. She wouldn't have helped me translate this or that passage of "Time Passes," just as I didn't help her write this or that chapter of a novel, but I would bring some of my worries to our conversations and she would wipe them away with a word or gesture.

The rain came in. But they never sent; never came.

La pluie entrait. No. La pluie pénétrait. That's better. Another problem: *they never sent*. An absolute construction, without an object. Impossible in French. Ils ne faisaient jamais signe? Ils ne donnaient aucune nouvelle? Ils n'envoyaient jamais personne? They gave no sign? They sent no news? They never sent anyone? La pluie pénétrait. Mais ils n'envoyaient jamais rien; ne venaient jamais. This is closer to the rhythm of the original.

Some of the locks had gone, so the doors banged.

Rain coming in, doors banging, signs of an unusual, inexplicable presence. There's no ghost in the sequence of words. Just a series of elements that have replaced human presence. Something that was out of place, that overstepped its rights and its role.

She didn't like to be up here alone at dusk either. It was too much for one woman, too much, too much. She creaked, she moaned. She banged the door. She turned the key in the lock, and left the house shut up, locked, alone.

Elle n'aimait pas non plus être seule là-bas au crépuscule. C'était trop pour une seule femme, beaucoup trop (trickier to repeat *trop, trop* than *too much, too much*). Elle craquait, gémissait. Everything is upside down. To *creak* would suit a door better than a human being, but words that usually refer to people are used for the elements, for nature, for parts of the house and words that normally apply to a house are now used for a woman.

With this the passage ends, and the fate of the house is sealed, left on its own.

More and more often, I would go to the Neustadt district, the new city district. I preferred the buildings from the last century with their blind walls repainted in modern colors, covered with graffiti and drawings. I preferred the inner courtyards and café terraces, the improvised flea markets or vendors' stalls stretching down to the river. I was reluctant to stay longer in the room that had welcomed me at first; I wondered if I should look for lodging on the other side of the river, even if I still went to the Kulturpalast café on my morning breaks so as to follow the Christmas-market preparations. Didn't looking for another room imply moving? And didn't I need—or was this just my superstition—the discomfort of being transient, of living in provisional circumstances to better understand the fate of the empty house? Also, I would secretly think, to receive the apparition that came to see me, since it preferred to stay close to the river?

Still, back in my room at night, I'd have liked to see a light across the way, lit windows showing me that I wasn't alone, that others were keeping watch, and that it would take just a few steps for me to stop in and visit a neighbor. Instead, all I could see from my window was the elegant silhouette of the gingko, whose leaves were turning evermore golden, a sliver of sky, and the river, whose proximity I could feel. It was because of this view that I had taken the room, but with time, it had begun to seem too empty of human presence. Compared to the liveliness of the cafés and ephemeral boutiques or in light of my sudden need for contact, the sky's austerity no longer held sway.

I looked, I searched—everything seemed connected. On some Internet search that I can't retrace, clicking from one site to another—because today, every site is a page on the Internet rather than a real place—I had come across Dunwich, a village on the Suffolk coast engulfed by the sea, or rather, a city of which only a few houses remain. Around 1830, Turner painted an astonishing watercolor depicting waves and spray beating against the cliffs, on the edge of which, in ghostly white, a church looms near a few vaguely drawn houses, all ruined, hinted at through the mixture of white and blue, which is characteristic of the sea and sky and visible through the empty structure of the church. (Experts point out that Turner had rotated the church 180 degrees to make it look like it was about to fall over the edge.) But what's most extraordinary is that the rounded shape of the cliff seems to meld with the wave, so that it looks like it's emerging from it or is part of it, unless it's the enormous back of a sea monster come to carry all the rest away.

Fifteen churches lie here
Under the North Sea;
Forty-five years ago
The last went down the cliff.

Anthony Thwaite. "At Dunwich." A poem written in 1963. Dunwich's heyday was in the twelfth century. But coastal erosion got the upper hand, and a succession of violent storms accelerated the process.

It seems that there is a whole series of poems about sunken cities in English literature, almost a genre of its own—could "Time Passes" be included in this tradition? The lighthouse may not be engulfed by the sea, but it is by time and circumstances—war and death. Isn't this as violent a devastation as the North Sea storms? Dunwich was the name of a fictional city in Massachusetts dreamed up by H. P. Lovecraft. Maybe the name was inspired by the Suffolk village. Lovecraft's Dunwich is dotted with abandoned houses in an architectural style that is strangely ancient compared to the other buildings, and the inhabitants are terrifying. In 1928, when Lovecraft conceived his long novella set in Dunwich and invented its features, Thwaite's poem didn't exist. Lovecraft could only have known Swinburne's 1880 poem, which begins with these lines:

A land that is lonelier than ruin
A sea that is stranger than death.

An opening that is fitting for the evocation of the fictional city in Massachusetts . . . Vanished, sunken cities, abandoned houses.

The house was left; the house was deserted.

The balance between the two exactly symmetrical parts of the phrase. La maison était laissée; la maison était désertée. But *laissée* doesn't work, it should be *délaissée* for a sense of abandonment. I was in the café with the large glass windows, there was no sense of abandonment around me. Quite the opposite: the city was animated in the run up to Christmas and the stands of the coming market would soon offer regional products, mulled wine to their strange residents—large figurines straight out of children's fairy tales.

It was left like a shell on a sandhill to fill with dry salt grains now that life had left it.

Délaissée comme un coquillage sur une dune de sable qui se remplissait de grains de sel desséchés maintenant que la vie l'avait quitté. *Délaissé*, *desséché* for *left*, *dry*, monosyllables that, when translated, overstep permitted limits, but what can you do? The sentence I'd just written seemed bloodless, without rhythm. Délaissée tel un coquillage sur la dune qui s'emplissait de grains de sel secs dès lors que la vie l'avait quitté. This is the beginning of the ninth sequence, the penultimate and longest one. The one in which the house is finally left to itself. At least at the start. The sequence in which everything could shift, the pivotal moment in the novel.

The long night seemed to have set in; the trifling airs, nibbling, the clammy breaths, fumbling, seemed to have triumphed.

I was not thrilled to see this sequence of present participles. Airy interior rhymes in English. Which would give what in French? La longue nuit semblait s'être installée; les airs anodins, grignotant, les souffles moites, tâtonnant, semblaient avoir triomphé. A disaster, as I expected. La longue nuit semblait s'être installée; les airs futiles, à force de ronger, les souffles moites, à force de tâtonner semblaient avoir triomphé. Hopeless. The sentence has grown much longer than Woolf's. How can I capture its sense of soaring, of flight—I must try to think about the text not as a sacrosanct monument but as a construction as human as it is literary, with all its weaknesses, and to accept the fact that its translation will be merely an imperfect approach. Today's attempt was anything but triumphant. And the bustle in the café, busier than usual, overlay the devastation on the page. What was going on? Was some group having a reunion? Several tables had been pushed together, and little by little—I looked up—the café was filling up. The noise grew louder while the sky's uniform gray announced the short December days.

The saucepan had rusted and the mat decayed. Toads had nosed their way in. Idly, aimlessly, the swaying shawl swung to and fro.

The first two sentences are straightforward, but the next one? Two words to describe an automatic, random movement, three others to describe the movement itself. *Swaying*, *swung*, and the adverb *to and fro*, designating a back-and-forth motion. Furthermore, all the words in this sentence are short, and *the swaying shawl swung to and fro* has a balanced rhythm of its own with every other syllable accented. I tried to distract myself from my discouragement by feigning interest in the group that was gathering a few tables from mine. Maybe they were musicians in the orchestra that was performing tonight? The organizers? The staff? They were greeting each other. These were men and women between thirty and fifty years old, their clothes indicated that they were well off, some had had a socialist upbringing, others had—how to put it, a liberal one? Some of them were perhaps from the West, others from the East, but they were meeting here, putting aside any differences they might have. Someone arrived who seemed to be the most important person of the gathering, because they fell silent and he sat at the place that had been reserved for him mid-table, which I hadn't noticed had remained empty, proof that I would be mediocre witness. I thought I had a feel for languages, but the number of imperfections I let pass until I had a better version later, disabused me of that. Not to mention the many assonances I didn't do anything with. So then, there was this shawl that swayed and swung, pointlessly moving to and fro. Sans raison, sans but, le châle oscillait en un mouvement de va-et-vient. Sans but, sans raison, le châle balançait, oscillant çà et là.

A thistle thrust itself between the tiles in the larder. The swallows nested in the drawing room; the floor was strewn with straw; the plaster fell in shovelfuls; rafters were laid bare; rats carried off this and that to gnaw behind the wainscots.

Un chardon s'immisçait dans le carrelage du garde-manger. Les hirondelles nichaient au salon; le sol était jonché de paille; le plâtre tombait par pelletées; il y avait des poutres à nu; des rats transportaient telle ou telle chose qu'ils rongeaient (qu'ils allaient ronger) derrière les lambris. How strange. A short sentence can resist for hours or weeks every attempt to transpose it, while a longer, apparently more complex sentence can be approached without opposition. Of course, this first version is far from perfect, but at least it doesn't have anything completely unmanageable.

Where is the memory of voices located? With effort, I could hear the intonations, the timbre of her voice, the expressions she used and the way she used them. I didn't have any of her books in Dresden. I'd brought only a few things with me, my indispensable laptop—I could almost have left with nothing but my laptop since it held all my work and much of my life—and a paperback edition of *To the Lighthouse*. A few changes of clothes and toiletries. That was enough for a few weeks or a few months. I had read somewhere, perhaps in an interview with Paul Virilio, that we should redefine the terms "sedentary" and "nomad." In our age of mobility, the sedentary one is the person who feels at home everywhere, and the nomad is the one who doesn't feel at home anywhere. Was I, then, sedentary or nomad? I felt sometimes like the one, sometimes like the other, and at that moment, in Dresden, I felt I was neither, but simply waiting for something—for someone.

Compared to the first version, the manuscript version, there were some additions and some deletions. Those that had been cut primarily served to connect two ideas, two passages, two ambiences. *So when she had gone*, it says in the manuscript, "she" referring to Mrs. McNab, *ill temperedly banging the doors, & forgetting her flowers, the house seemed like a shell deserted of life, & given over to moulder on a sandhill.*

In the Uniform edition, it says, *It was left like a shell on a sandhill to fill with dry salty grains now that life had left it.*

The shell, the neglect, the sandhill, and the absence of life remain but the order is upended and Mrs. McNab's abandonment is transformed into a universal one. In the transition from the manuscript version to the Uniform edition, it's often the human presence that is erased, the text gains a more metaphorical tone, underscored by the shifting of certain words, through which the striking imagery of the first description is replaced with more complex connections and associations. Still, even if the first version is on the whole simpler, or rather, a more immediate one, it does contain the idea of a world order overturned, the description of a chaos that is not apocalyptic but caused by slight displacements, like the shawl swaying on its own, which suggests an autonomous life, especially with the airs and breaths preceding it—a ghostly presence. The animal and plant worlds have crept into a space usually reserved for humans and in reading, in translating the rusted saucepan, I pictured the rusted automobiles, the forever immobilized bumper cars of Pripyat, and in this sequence of words I particularly recalled the voiceovers in the documentaries filmed in the exclusion zone—deserted, abandoned, devoid of all human presence. And I fantasized that one day it would occur to someone to show a series of images of foxes or wolves on the watch in the forest, of birds flying over empty waterways, of fruits left unpicked accompanied by the entirety of "Time Passes" in voiceover. The text would not be an illustration of the images any more than the images would be a commentary on the text; each would bear witness to the same catastrophe, to a premonition of humanity's fate.

The sound of a voice that returns in moments when we don't expect it because a similar intonation or a word recalls a past conversation. Here in Dresden, they speak a language that is neither the language of our conversations nor the one I am translating, it's a language that is like an island where I could find refuge, far from my life—apart from my life—an island from which I saw the usual waves that moved the sea and broke on the shore but from another vantage point, in an attempt to protect myself, to not remember so often, to avoid the memories. Here no one asked anything of me. I had no role to play. I was an anonymous passerby whose voice no one knew.

Returning one evening from the Neustadt district, where I had looked at several small apartments, none of which had convinced me, returning via the bridge from which I had a view of the spires and towers and their lights reflected in the river, coming back from a silent walk during which images of the exclusion zone mingled with the words of "Time Passes," which I now knew by heart, I passed a group of students and overheard a few words. And I thought I heard—no, I was sure I heard—someone say with a laugh, So you believe in ghosts? The question floated, unmoored, not connected either to the preceding sentence or leading to the next because they were walking quickly, and by the time I realized what I'd heard, it was too late to turn around, and the cold discouraged me from following them. In the next instant, a silhouette was approaching me and the following happened—how to put it—without my intervention. I experienced, I witnessed—how can I describe the sensation of being sucked into a time, into a reality I couldn't have imagined minutes before. A silhouette, a shade, a vague form with vague contours that I thought I recognized. Is it you? I asked although I wasn't speaking—although I didn't hear the sound of my voice. Me, the form said.

The sea—are you still looking for it?

I'm not looking.

What are you doing?

Remembering.

You remember?

I'm searching.

In your memory?

I'm coming.

Where are you?

You see me.

But before?

There's no name.

And you?

No name.

Then nothing more, and then nothing. It was a nameless experience, a kind of encounter or mental state, that may not have even occurred.

INTERLUDE

On the High Line, bridges and tunnels alternate. Some people talk of parks, of forests—isn't that an exaggeration? But why not see the whole of the universe in this stretch of elevated track the way you can see it in a Japanese garden? Bridges and tunnels, tunnels and bridges. Under the High Line, museums, galleries, and installations are multiplying. Art is demanding its rights. It's not enough to present the world, it must also be represented. Graffiti and paintings, heaps of material sorted by color or density to the sound of repetitive music or a Joni Mitchell song. "Both Sides Now." "I've looked at life from both sides now, from win and lose . . . ," she says, "I've looked at clouds from both sides now, from up and down . . . "

The High Line rises above the city, but still belongs to it like those alternative spaces that both call the norm into question and reinforce it, which in turn maintains it. The underground never lasts long. Word of it spreads *sotto voce*, rumors of it become audible, artists move in, making their homes in places no would have considered livable, then bit by bit, everything changes. The artists show their works in garages, in basements, in apartments furnished with salvaged things, whether in countries with political censorship or in those with economic censorship—what we call the "law of the market"—and the curious come, then collectors, gallerists, investors, and suddenly luxury apartment buildings rise, lining the High Line on the side of the Hudson River. In a matter of months, these buildings fill a horizon of once vast, open expanses. How can one imagine, standing on the escalators in this shopping center filled with expensive brands, that not long ago there was nothing here? Where did the people crowding into that café, or lingering over a cocktail, or savoring a hamburger go before? What did they do when, instead of the Hudson Yards, there were just empty lots and train tracks leading to Penn Station? Each place creates its own necessity, each place creates its own newcomers, its residents—everyone always comes from elsewhere . . . The flow of arrivals and departures is endless even if, up on the High Line, people prefer to pause—on the wooden benches integrated into the entirety of the landscape like rows of seats in ancient theaters, on which resting passersby become spectators waiting for the entrance of actors, who themselves are other passersby. Is it Joni Mitchell's voice, lower than usual, rising vaguely from the urban sea to confide to us that she is looking at clouds from both sides now . . . We see the clouds on the High Line, and we may think we are closer to them than on the streets below, but the buildings that sprout continuously push them away into a sky that is less and less accessible.

VI

Maybe you have to be at a certain elevation to see a city, to take it in. Maybe you have to climb a tower or a hill to get an overview of its topography, the shape of its contours and surroundings, its expanse. Maybe it's reassuring to see that there is a limit, that the city does not extend into infinity but is encircled by wooded hills, that it abuts the sea, that it ends somewhere. We still hear the noise of the city, but nothing reveals its activity. And you have to climb down again, to mix with the passersby, and walk through its streets to know a city's heart, its breath, its very being. I had been in Dresden for weeks, and yet had only recently become aware of the effects it can have. Outwardly, my life here looked the same as my life in Paris. But the strangers in the streets were not the same, the language I heard around me was not the same, and instead of believing, as I had, that it made no difference, that I was living in exactly the same way and doing the same work, I began to realize that I too was being changed. Just as the gingko with golden leaves that filled me with happiness had replaced the series of zinc roofs in Paris, my internal visions had modified me, and what I encountered, what was offered to me, had an influence. Who knows whether I would have chosen different words for my translation if I'd remained at my usual work desk? Who can say what thoughts would have occurred to me, what associations or blocks or solutions?

Coleridge's story about the composition the origin of his poem "Kubla Khan" goes as follows: waking from a vision-filled sleep, he began to write them down but was interrupted by a knock on his door. He rose to answer and was detained for over an hour by a person who had come on business from Porlock. By the time Coleridge returned to his poem, he had all but forgotten what he wanted to write. Hence the poem remained a mere fragment. "A person from Porlock" has come to mean any kind of interruption for those who know this anecdote. In order to come to Dresden, I'd interrupted the course of my life without knowing that nothing could again be as before.

—"Profoundly calm (in a sweetly sonorous fog)." These markings follow the title on the score of *The Sunken Cathedral*, the tenth of Debussy's piano *Préludes, Book One*, which he composed in 1910 about the mythical city of Ys that was engulfed by the sea.

—They say that bells are sometimes heard ringing there.

—This piece of music, written for solo piano, is around six and a half minutes long. At measure sixteen, Debussy gives the following instruction: *peu à peu sortant de la brume* (emerging from the fog little by little). Other markings, purely pianistic ones, follow: "gradually becoming louder, sonorous without harshness, floating and muted, like an echo of the preceding phrase."

—They say that the cathedral is first evoked underwater. We sense the sound of the bells. Then the cathedral emerges, the tolling of the bells becomes more intense. Then it disappears again. It's also the rhythm of the legend.

—In a letter to Henry Malherbe, Claude Debussy wrote, "Who can know the secret of musical composition? The sound of the sea, the line of a horizon, the wind in the leaves, the cry of a bird leave in us varied impressions. And suddenly, completely without our consent, one of these memories emerges from us, expressing itself in the language of music."

—Who can say what echoes works of music will create in us? What mysterious resonances? What unknown correspondences will arise when we hear them?

—Ceri Richards, a painter who was born in Wales in 1903 and died in 1971, spent nearly a decade painting a series of sunken cathedrals inspired by Debussy's musical markings.

—The series *La Cathédrale engloutie* (*profondément calme*) is painted entirely in shades of blue. Abstract shapes, a marine sky. Below, rectangles and circles build a balancing edifice.

—Then red appears. Sonorous but without harshness. Some recollections of blue.

—The city of Ys is just one of many engulfed by the sea. And on the coast of the North Sea and that of the Baltic, on the islands or on the mainland, it's the bells that warn of imminent disaster; they ring until it's too late—the last vestiges of a human life.

Tortoise-shell butterflies burst from the chrysalis and pattered their life out on the window-pane.

Pattered out suggests a kind of extension, of expansion, something directed toward life that prolonged their emergence from the chrysalis. Another observation that recalls the moth banging against the windowpane. Here we are at the beginning of life, the window is a fortunate testing ground. A few years later, it becomes a cemetery of attempts to live.

Poppies sowed themselves among the dahlias; the lawn waved with long grass; giant artichokes towered among roses; a fringed carnation flowered among the cabbages; while the gentle tapping of a weed at the window had become, on winters' nights, a drumming from sturdy trees and thorned briars which made the whole room green in summer.

It is the center of the devastation, all the more alarming and tragic for being described in almost innocuous, harmless words. *Long grass* not tall grass? *Sowed themselves.* Had sown themselves. There's no longer any need for human intervention—the plants and flowers are growing of their own accord. Poppies were sowing themselves among the dahlias.

From now on, I won't be able to help thinking of a catastrophe of any dimension only in these terms: an artichoke among roses. This image did not occur to Virginia Woolf immediately. In the Berg manuscript, after describing the beds and seats overgrown with vegetation, she initially wrote: *sudden beauty flower in the midst of chaos—a rare rose, or a fine carnation.*

The first vision was of general chaos punctuated here and there with traces of beauty. In the later version, the inversion—the description of a single disruptive element in the midst of beauty—had a symbolic, metaphorical value, and was much more powerful.

That is when I started to think of those I'd left behind in Paris, whose messages and calls I'd ignored, having brought with me only a sense of loss.

In this city, where no one knew me, where I didn't know anyone, I suddenly understood the importance of names. I recalled the names of those close to me, and the memories and emotions associated with them. I suddenly wanted to see them all; I wanted to hug my parents, my brother, whom I almost never saw, my sister, whom I saw more often, my friends, to whom I hadn't even bothered sending a text message to let them know I was leaving. That evening, I was about to call someone, to click randomly on a contact and then on the telephone icon, an act that was almost abstract. It was enough to press a spot on my phone and I would hear a voice, all at once the familiar world that had faded would return in force and I'd no longer be able to bear being in Dresden. I couldn't give in to temptation, I'd call later when it was time to return to Paris. To resist the pull, I did some random searches on the Internet, then entered two names: Virginia Woolf and Dresden.

At first, all I found were announcements of several performances of Edward Albee's play, *Who's Afraid of Virginia Woolf?*, in a Dresden theater. Then I found traces of a trip that Virginia, when her name was still Stephen, had taken with her brother Adrian in August 1909, after a stay in Bayreuth. She wasn't particularly taken with the paintings, and she and her brother saw a production of Richard Strauss's *Salome* at the opera house: a discovery, she wrote and, immediately tempering her reaction, described as emotion without beauty. Then I came across a phrase from *To the Lighthouse* about Lily Briscoe, the painter: "She had been to Dresden; there were masses of pictures she had not seen." In the following sentence, Lily Briscoe reflects that "perhaps it was better not to see pictures: they only made one hopelessly discontented with one's own work." Dresden is evoked only by name. Mr. Bankes had been to Amsterdam and Madrid, while Lily Briscoe had been to Brussels, to Paris, and to Dresden. Somewhat more unsettling, Virginia Stephen writes her address in the header of a letter to her sister Vanessa Bell, Prager Strasse 38. Of course, this was before the bombardment, but also before Otto Dix's painting, before the chaos of the two world wars. Prager Strasse had been a prestigious street in Dresden at the time, as its Wikipedia page confirms. The street's principal function was to connect the newly built train station to the city. I learned that, thanks to its reconstruction, it became one of the first pedestrian zones in Germany.

Woolf was not particularly interested in Germany, which nonetheless was one of the first countries to translate her works. *To the Lighthouse* was translated into German in 1931, preceded by *Mrs. Dalloway*, which oddly became *A Woman of Fifty*, and *Orlando*. She was less drawn to Germany than she was to France and Italy or to the Russian language and literature. And Nazism didn't help. But to go from Holland to Italy and despite warnings from the Foreign Office—Leonard Woolf's family was Jewish—Leonard and Virginia Woolf crossed Germany by car—three days of travel in May 1935. Her diary bears traces of this strange sojourn. The account begins on May 9 with Virginia's worry when Leonard had been inside the customs building for ten minutes, whereas on the Dutch side the formalities had been taken care of in ten seconds. But Leonard soon came out. The couple was traveling with a marmoset and that, apparently, is what saved them from the abyss. The customs officers looked at it fondly, as did the crowd waiting for Göring to drive past, who then gave the Woolfs' car and their marmoset Mitzi an enthusiastic Hitler salute. The days were tense, filled with obsequiousness and anger according to the diary, which also records the phrases on the banners: "The Jew is our enemy," "There is no place for Jews in—". The next entry is dated May 12. Although the entry of May 8 indicates Utrecht and that of May 12 Innsbruck, the entry noting their passage through Germany strangely does not bear a place name, as if it were nowhere. The Innsbruck entry—the return of the city's name is like a return to the world—opens with these lines: "L. says I may now tell the truth, but I have forgotten 2 days of truth, & my pen is weeping ink." The Rhine, the Neckar, Heidelberg, the university, Augsburg—a dull city but they had a room with a bath. Every village had the sign "*Juden sind hier unwunscht*" (she no doubt meant *unerwünscht*). Jews are not welcome.

What power could now prevent the fertility, the insensibility of nature? Mrs. McNab's dream of a lady, of a child, of a plate of milk soup?

Le rêve de Mrs. McNab d'une dame, d'un enfant, d'une assiette de soupe au lait? The apostrophe in the English possessive form makes it possible to avoid repeating the preposition as is necessary in French and to distinguish the dreamer from the subject of her dream. Or would it be better to say: le rêve de Mrs. McNab au sujet d'une dame, the dream Mrs. McNab had about a woman . . . no, too cumbersome. Or: quand Mrs. McNab rêve d'une dame . . . when Mrs. McNab dreams of a woman . . . And wouldn't rêverie work better than rêve?

It had wavered over the walls like a spot of sunlight and vanished. She had locked the door; she had gone.

This entire passage takes up the preceding sequence again, returning to Mrs. McNab's vision of Mrs. Ramsay. So, the human presence was nothing more than a reverie, a vision—a memory.

It was beyond the strength of one woman, she said. They never sent. They never wrote.

It was not beyond the strength of *a* woman, but of *one* woman. Then additional variations on the previous occurrences. Ils n'envoyaient rien? Ils n'envoyaient personne? N'écrivaient pas. They never sent anything? They never sent anyone? Never wrote. Or rather: Ils n'écrivaient jamais. They never wrote.

There were things up there rotting in the drawers—it was a shame to leave them so, she said. The place was gone to rack and ruin.

Now I was waiting for her. I wanted to see her. Maybe waiting was a mistake because she didn't come. Sent no sign. Unless my memories were signs, because their flow was constant: scenes I thought I'd forgotten, comments I occasionally wondered if I'd perhaps made up, things said on a walk after lunch on the way to a bus stop. I pictured places at the same time as I heard her voice. The words could not be separated from the places where they'd been said, where I thought they'd been said. For example, in a narrow street in the center of Paris, passing a church, the name of which I've forgotten, she had spoken of an evening event during which someone was discussing a book in a way that made her think at first that he was the author until a remark he made detached him from the text and through that gap she perceived that he was the translator, not the author. She couldn't remember the remark. She only remembered that he hadn't mentioned the author's name until she asked. And as I walked around the construction site, enclosed by a fence that hid it from view—you could see the machine's arms regularly rise and hear the sound of invisible work—as I walked around the construction site in Dresden, the Parisian street became superimposed on it, without any connection or reason other than the synchronicity of my thoughts.

That night I fell asleep late, waiting for something, a vision, her arrival. Waiting is a state that is not easy to emerge from, it takes over your entire being—body and mind—and does not yield. I learned to live with the longing for a vision like all those who weep in secret, like the silent souls who are filled with regret. But no visit came to fill my nightly vigils.

Only "Time Passes" sent signals—the lighthouse beam that spun, illuminating neglected areas here and there.

—The sound of bells, Rachmaninoff said, dominated all the cities of Russia I used to know. They accompanied every Russian from childhood to the grave. Is that why he composed *The Bells, Kolokola*, a symphonic poem for choir, voice, and orchestra based on Edgar Allan Poe's poem? Four movements, four ages. The cheerfulness of sleighbells in childhood, the melodic solemnity of wedding bells, the fear sparked by alarm bells, then the somber tones of the death knell.

—Maybe it was the death knell of the old Russia and the old Europe that heralded the loss of a world, the millions of war dead, he implied.

—In exile in America, Rachmaninoff also said that in losing Russia, he lost himself. He left behind his desire to compose.

Only the Lighthouse beam entered the rooms for a moment, sent its sudden stare over bed and wall in the darkness of winter, looked with equanimity at the thistle and the swallow, the rat and the straw.

Seul le rayon du phare pénétrait dans les chambres un instant, lançait sa fixité soudaine sur le lit et le mur dans l'obscurité de l'hiver, regardait avec sérénité—serenity? Or should I keep equanimity?—le chardon et l'hirondelle, le rat et la paille. It sounds better with the order reversed. Regardait avec équanimité l'hirondelle et le chardon, la paille et le rat. The only gaze in this universe is the lighthouse's, reinforcing its secret connection with Mrs. Ramsay. In the very first version, the Berg manuscript, there is a passage about the people who had been walking the beach, looking for an answer to their doubts, and who, in falling asleep, abandoned their bodies for their dreams. This passage came after the lighthouse beam. But in later versions, humanity has disappeared from the house and, for a time, from the world, and the final version took up the thread later.

Nothing now withstood them; nothing said no to them. Let the wind blow; let the poppy seed itself and the carnation mate with the cabbage. Que le vent souffle; que le coquelicot se sème et que l'oeillet s'accouple au chou. Le coquelicot se sème. Sounds without harmony. Is it significant that it is the poppy, the flower that in England commemorates the dead in the First World War? *Let the poppy seed itself.* It's important to keep the impersonal form and not bring in any agency with the first- or second-person plural: laissons le vent souffler or laissez le vent souffler.

Looking out the café window at the Christmas market, which was now open—since time was passing—I searched in vain for an impersonal way to express the imperative that would avoid the repetition of *que* for let (que le vent souffle . . .). But I couldn't find a solution and was distracted by the traffic on the street and the tramcars. It was a day when the real landscape was more substantial than the book, when I was not able to withdraw from my surroundings and dive toward the lighthouse. Watching the customers entering and leaving the café, more than once I thought I recognized someone,

someone who couldn't be there or whose presence was very improbable. While I refused all contact with those I'd left behind—there was now a hint of exasperation in the voice messages and texts on my phone—I did call them mentally, summoning them to Dresden to visit me. I addressed them as a group to cover the presence of the person I was thinking of with presences that were less important to me. Finally, I closed my laptop.

There was no point continuing and I left through the hall of the Kulturpalast. At the ticket counter, there were thick concert schedules. I took one and leafed through it idly, sitting on a bench. That same evening there was a concert with—and this caught my attention—Mendelssohn's *Hebrides Overture*, also called *Fingal's Cave*, in which the composer transcribed his impressions of a trip to the island of Staffa in Scotland with its famous cave, basalt columns, and narrow water passages. The final version was written in 1832 with a certain number of revisions to the version of 1830, perhaps reflected in the change of titles—the original title was *The Lonely Island*. The program explained that this piece is generally considered a milestone in the Romantic tradition. I could not pass up the opportunity to hear this overture, which opened only onto itself and struck me as a foreshadowing of "Time Passes" with its similar setting, an imagined island off the coast of Scotland, with the same elements, the sea and the wind, and similar revisions over an extended process of creation. There were a few tickets left and I bought one without checking which other pieces were on the program, intending to leave after hearing the Mendelssohn. I vaguely remembered that there was a symphony in the second half by a nineteenth-century composer, Bruckner or Brahms, of little interest to me. I managed to translate a few more sentences in the afternoon, but my thoughts wandered.

Let the swallow build in the drawing-room, and the thistle thrust aside the tiles, and the butterfly sun itself on the faded chintz of the arm-chairs.

The same elements appeared but in a different order. Que l'hirondelle construise dans le salon, et le chardon . . . If I used the subjunctive puisse, it would avoid the repetition of Que, but wouldn't that be overinterpreting it? Puisse l'hirondelle bâtir au salon, et le chardon écarter le carrelage . . . , may the swallow build in the drawing-room, and the thistle thrust aside the tiles . . .

Let the broken glass and the china lie out on the lawn and be tangled over with grass and wild berries.

Puisse le verre cassé et la porcelaine—nothing was working and I was too distracted to find a solution. Next was a pivotal passage that demanded my complete concentration, and it was getting late. I'd have to put it off until tomorrow.

It was dark when I set out, of course. I had worked on the last lines with the lights on. I walked quickly, not only because the temperature had dropped significantly with the approach of winter, but mostly because I had the sense that I was heading to a rendezvous. For the first time since I'd settled temporarily in Dresden, I was going somewhere intentionally, with a plan. It was if I had to meet someone.

The concert hall was a kind of amphitheater. The red of the seats, less intense than in the Italian-style halls, harmonized with the off-white walls and ceilings. The amphitheater, unusually, had angles and broken lines and, I'd read, more than 1,700 seats. I arrived early. I liked watching the hall fill, hearing the hubbub swell gradually, and waiting for the moment when the lights were turned off and silence would fall. Miraculously, I had a good seat, in the center of a row facing the orchestra, in the first group, colored in green on the seating map of the hall, but at an affordable price. The seats next to me were still empty, as was the stage. I'd paused briefly on my way to the hall in front of the large mural that had escaped from the socialist regime—there had been plans to tear down the building and, before the murals were designated as cultural heritage, they had been largely taken down. Conservation was begun only much later. I'd stopped before this hymn to workers, to the red banner, to the history of the workers movement in which a woman led the march like Delacroix's *Liberty Leading the People*. Then I entered the building that had also survived recent history and the regime change, and I watched the audience as it began to stream in, trying to imagine that I belonged to this city like they did, thinking that for them, I was just one person among many, a Dresden resident, the same as I saw them, although there probably was someone among them who was as much a stranger as I, or maybe even more of a stranger. Did they want to live where they did? Did some of them wish they could spend a few weeks in another city, in another country, where they could blend in, unknown, into an anonymous crowd and indulge in the illusion that they belonged?

The hall was filling. I enjoy that moment of anticipation, when all questions are suspended, when, as on a train or airplane journey, we have given up all responsibility—everything occurs before our eyes, but outside of us. The hall was filling, the seats were gradually being occupied, and I'd stood up several times to let someone pass, but there was still no one next to me. Watching the audience members walk down the aisle, I tried to guess from their gait or their expression who would sit next to me. And then, they arrived. On one side was a man with a group of friends, middle-aged like me, and on the other a woman I didn't notice right away because I was looking at the audience behind and above me. The concert was about to begin, the chimes were ringing. I looked to my left, the woman had just taken her seat, the lights went out at that same moment, but something nagged at me, a vision, an emotion, the sense that I knew the person I'd just glimpsed—and as silence fell, I suddenly saw the friend I'd lost. She had taken on the features of the person sitting next to me. Or they looked alike. Or I thought of her at that moment. Something was calling to her—in the darkness of the hall, in the movement of the musicians getting ready.

The first measures of the *Hebrides Overture* resounded—blankets of sound that evoked the bare, desolate expanses of the Scottish islands, with their shades of brown and green bordered by the sea. I tried to sink into the music and forget the unease that had come over me, to submerge myself in the rising water, in the flood of notes. Leafing through the program, I'd read that the first theme came to Mendelssohn when he was visiting Fingal's Cave, that he had inscribed a few notes in a letter to his sister Fanny. I tried to dive into the sounds of the viola, the cello, the bassoon, to let myself be overwhelmed by the mix of strings and woodwinds, to be transported, but some part of me remained in the hall, or rather, in a feeling of loss, and it was this feeling that spread, that expanded, that threatened to swallow me. Invisible presences trembled in the darkness, each one had brought its own world, its absences, its ghosts, that floated freely from one to another—I was haunted by unknown beings, or beings who seemed unknown. Maybe they did, in fact, come from the Hebrides, but they seemed, rather, to come from the city's past and from their own in order to encircle my past and the life that I had wanted to put on hold and that they were now swallowing, while I, as if clinging to a raft carrying me against the current, tried to save my past and become one with myself again. I tried to remember buried names, to run through bad events, to get back on course.

Silence fell, applause rang out. The *Hebrides Overture* I had come for was finished without my really having heard it. The conductor bowed before the applause died down again. I heard someone breathing next to me. I didn't dare look, fearing that in the darkness I would recognize the friend I had lost. A low, unfamiliar tone made me shudder. Long, sustained notes. A bass clarinet, the music was accompanied by a breath.

Without trying to understand what was happening, I let it carry me, not knowing if I was heading toward the past or the future. An image appeared, a shadow on a white wall, blurred and unmoving, I or someone else battled against the wait. Or rather, it was like an aquatic universe that was spreading, barely audible notes, minute variations, a ship's horn suddenly sounded a departure, water, sustained notes and something rising and calling, a mystery playing out on moving lines, a dive to the depths, the call repeats and lingers insistently. Mysterious and dense, an exploration, a repeated, captivating dive, layers of water part, something rises, nearly inaudible but tenacious, it vibrates and returns. Occasionally there was a bell-like sound, muffled chimes that restrained their sound, or a sound like a foghorn on top of a lighthouse over the open sea, a heartbeat. Silence. And it all begins again differently, things resound more clearly, more sonorous and higher arpeggios, a continuing call, like a voice, a cry from the depths of time, pure time, its miniscule variations, its occasional immobility, the motion of the waves, an ebb and flow, the past, the present, blending and becoming indistinguishable in a low harmony from which always comes the same call, a discreet and elegant distress call in which life is multiplied and becomes more complex. Meteoric passages, ephemeral flashes like shades on a pastel-colored cloth, arrows shot at silence.

I wasn't listening, I was enthralled. I was no longer separate from the music, I had become one with it, or it had entered into me and in that moment of silence, I was suspended.

And then the density of the notes, solid ground on which to come ashore, shallows uncovered at low tide. The people walking the beach looking for an answer to their question. The question is asked and ascends. The presences whirl and spin around it, something encircles us. Did I see the face of a soul? Is she seated next to me? Should I speak to her, ignore her? Wait for a sign from her? The music, now calmer, stops again. Then a storm roars, something emerging from the deep. Calm returns, but provisionally, only for an instant, in fragile equilibrium. The wind rises, the storm has burst or the dive into the water descends lower still—will we be able to return to the surface? Flashes speed past—colorful denizens of the deep sea. Nothing retains, nothing is retained. I see the flash, I hear the mystery that calls, the openings, the closings, the failed efforts, attempts to live, the call sounds again, the gravity, the precariousness of the conclusive, the poverty of our hopes. The vigilance, call and response, coastlines receding from view, the weight, the hope of a departure and an arrival, and the idea that life might finally defeat . . . the final silence.

The applause rang out and reminded me that this was a piece of music. I did as the others and applauded, but it was a meagre reaction compared to the journey that had left me washed up on the sand, castaway on the island like Odysseus or Robinson Crusoe, not knowing where I was, what to do, regaining consciousness with the sea and its dangers, the sea and its beauties as my only memory. I was glad for the intermission. I would be able to go out to the foyer—the light and the crowd dispersed my strange state somewhat—look at the program and put a name to the experience I had just had: *Coral de Caracola*, a magnificently sonorous name, full of mystery. As for the composer, his name was Juan Allende-Blin.

I had come this far. I had reached the very core, trying to forget who I was, where I came from, and where I was—at the café's large window, the Christmas market I found so appealing, passersby from early morning on, people in a hurry, who still paused and stole a few moments from their obligations and work to dream. I tried to forget everything beyond the lighthouse, the abandoned house, and time.

For now had come that moment, that hesitation when dawn trembles and night pauses, when if a feather alight in the scale it will be weighed down.

The idea is in the original manuscript and the beginning is almost identical, but in the final version, the rest of the phrase is amplified, made poetical, absolute. Car maintenant était venu ce moment, cette hésitation où l'aube tremble et où la nuit s'arrête, où si une plume posée sur l'échelle, elle sera alourdie. Nothing seemed right in this initial attempt. First of all, should I keep the odd construction, *if a feather alight in the scale*, in which alight seems to be functioning as a verb even though it's merely a participle, or should I simplify the syntax? Then there's that *weighed down*. Of course, the image is expressive. What if a floating feather falls? In French, scale is *échelle* or ladder. I pictured the feather hovering over a rung of the ladder but couldn't figure out why the preposition was *in* and not *on*. Something can't fall in a ladder. Checking the dictionary, I saw that in French, scale also means balance, a pair of scales, not just *échelle*. I quickly deleted the absurd ladder. Without it, the sentence was back in balance. Car maintenant venait le moment, l'hésitation lorsque l'aube tremble et que la nuit s'arrête, lorsqu'une plume posée sur la balance—naturally, I also had to replace dans, in, with sur, on—la ferait basculer. But I was working around the syntax of the original by avoiding the problem it was causing me. Changing the verb tense was not an easy way out, the sequence of tenses was different for each language. Turning the demonstrative adjective into a definite article wasn't a solution either, sometimes it was the opposite: definite in English, demonstrative in French. I still couldn't understand why *alight* appeared in this form and not in the simple past or past participle *alighted* as it does in the Berg manuscript which reads *if a feather had blown* with *blown* crossed out and replaced with *alighted*. I'd also have understood the old form of the simple past *alit*. But it says *alight* and I was getting lost in conjectures. If the verb were in the present tense it would have an s, *if a feather alights* . . . After a long search through grammar websites, I finally found the trace of the subjunctive. Of course, the subjunctive after *if*—obvious when you're saying *if I were*, but almost invisible here . . . Et maintenant venait le moment, l'hésitation où l'aube tremble et la nuit fait pause, où si une plume se déposait sur le plateau, celui-ci basculerait. A compromise so that I could continue.

One feather, and the house, sinking, falling, would have turned and pitched downwards to the depths of darkness.

To the Lighthouse, 1927. Invert two digits and you have 1972, the year the meteorologist Edward Lorenz gave his presentation on the butterfly effect. More precisely, the title of his paper was "Predictability: Does the Flap of a Butterfly's Wings in Brazil Set Off a Tornado in Texas?" Or the effect of small changes on large-scale phenomena, or the limits of predictability, or an explanation of chaos theory. But some fifty years earlier, the feather fell onto a scale pan and tipped it downward. And the scale determined the equilibrium of the world, or at least the world around the lighthouse. The consequences were listed, described in detail, picnickers would have come into the house to light their kettles, lovers would have sought shelter there, the shepherd eaten his dinner, and the tramp warded off the cold. Humankind would reappear in defiance of ownership and enter where it had no right, a humanity consisting of pariahs, transient visitors, picnickers, lovers, shepherds, tramps, all of them marginal compared with the forever absent owners, before vegetation in the form of brambles and hemlock took complete control of it. Only a few fragments of china, like those found in archeological digs, would testify to a human presence in remote times.

If the feather had fallen, if it had tipped the scale downwards, the whole house would have plunged to the depths to lie upon the sands of oblivion.

This sentence is almost exactly the same in the manuscript version. It is only missing the sands of oblivion and the sands of oblivion might lead to the assumption that the house had sunk into the sea, like the church painted by Turner on the cliff edge and on the verge of toppling.

But there was a force working; something not highly conscious; something that leered, something that lurched; something not inspired to go about its work with dignified ritual or solemn chanting.

Mais il y avait une force au travail; quelque chose qui n'était pas très conscient; quelque chose qui lorgnait (not an attractive word. And wouldn't une force à l'œuvre be better than au travail?) Mais il y avait une force à l'œuvre; quelque chose qui n'était pas grandement conscient; quelque chose qui scrutait, qui titubait; quelque chose qui n'était pas enclin à aller travailler avec un digne rituel ou un chant solennel. The rhythm is off . . . quelque chose qui scrutait, titubait. Quelque chose qui lorgnait (why not, after all, leered isn't attractive either), titubait . . . Quelque chose qui n'incitait pas à aller travailler dans un rituel digne ou avec un chant solennel. Make it simpler? Quelque chose qu'un digne rituel ou un chant solennel n'incitait pas à aller au travail.

—In countries with turbulent histories, there is something on the prowl, something lethal, and innocent travelers are caught in its snares.

—We see empty landscapes. But where is this place? A country where they speak of skulls and pale blue bones under the moon, where they speak of the dead, where nature is peaceful and humans are cruel.

—A nocturnal landscape, tall grass, a tree. Columns in the snow slide across a white screen set up in the night. They are alone, buried far from each other; they cannot rest in peace.

—Who is it? Who's speaking? Family pictures punctuate a model of nature—a model representing the world.

—Those who have disappeared wander the seabed.

—*Graves Without a Name* is the title of the film. More than a title, more than a film. The communication we seek to establish with the dead, the disappeared—those it was impossible to honor properly with a final ceremony.

—Rithy Panh is the director's name; *The Missing Picture* is another of his films.

—Nothing can kill a man, someone says. So many signs remain, so many thoughts arise, so many wandering souls who call to us, who wait for us—silhouettes that live among the branches, that live on stalks resembling a shadow theater.

—There are so few images at our disposal. This solitary tree in the middle of a field, it's Caspar David Friedrich's *Oak in the Snow*, even though there is no snow. And yet, the image travels in Europe, in Asia.

Humankind reappears in the form of two women tasked with suppressing the chaos and re-establishing order.

Mrs. McNab groaned. Mrs. Bast creaked.

These verbs aren't necessarily used with humans, one of them not even with living creatures. Mrs. Bast could be a door, Mrs. McNab an animal.

They were old; they were stiff; their legs ached.

What are they doing there? The answer is in the next sentence, as unexpected as the letter they'd received after so many years.

They came with their brooms and pails at last; they got to work.

Mrs. Bast has emerged from the void and come to help Mrs. McNab because it was too much work for one woman. *At last* sums up all the time that has passed.

All of a sudden, would Mrs. McNab see that the house was ready, one of the young ladies wrote: would she get this done; would she get that done; all in a hurry.

The news comes as unexpectedly to the reader of the novel as it does to Mrs. McNab. *All of a sudden. All in a hurry.* The family has left the brackets to return to the foreground. The reestablishment of order is now the agenda. The restoration of the nature of things or something that seems like it. The moment has passed; the feather did not fall. But Virginia Woolf does not say this. The conditional is enough. Even in the first version, the characters emerge without warning. There was, of course, a point to this turn of events but there was also a force working. And that force—along with destiny keeping watch and the young ladies taking up their lives again and their inheritance in the same way that the world, after the war, was taking up its course again and the inheritance of times past—that force was Mrs. McNab, on whom they suddenly called.

They might be coming for the summer; had left everything to the last; expected to find things as they had left them. Slowly and painfully, with broom and pail, mopping, scouring, Mrs. McNab, Mrs. Bast stayed the corruption and the rot; rescued from the pool of Time that was fast closing over them now a basin, now a cupboard; fetched from oblivion all the Waverley novels and a tea-set one morning; in the afternoon restored to sun and air a brass fender and a set of steel fire-irons.

One could say that Mrs. McNab and Mrs. Bast were poor in spirit—in the manuscript version, they were barely aware there had been a war—and yet, they are the ones charged with reestablishing balance, with ensuring the final onslaught and victory of the forces of cleanliness and symmetry over disarray. And their mission was a dangerous one, which they undertook courageously, like the soldiers who had gone into combat.

Literature, too, reappears. It had kept watch with Virgil and Mr. Carmichael and was the first sign of civilization to resurface, saved from oblivion at the last minute in the guise of Sir Walter Scott's Waverley novels. Far removed from Woolf and yet not so far. Sir Walter Scott had come to the Isle of Skye, where *To the Lighthouse* is set, and on a journey along the coast of Scotland, he had inspected lighthouses, a tour he described in a journal of "Northern Lights," which Virginia Stephen learned about at the age of fifteen when reading Lockhart's biography of Scott. Virginia Woolf wrote about Scott several decades later as "perhaps the last novelist to practice the great, the Shakespearean art, of making people reveal themselves in speech."

It was time for me to collect the scattered fragments of my evenings and days. I had to try to recall the continuity that had once governed my life. I walked along the aisles of the Christmas market; night had fallen in the middle of the afternoon, presaging a long cloak of darkness that would cover the city. I hadn't moved out of my apartment, I had stopped looking for a new one, I wasn't sure if I would stay in Dresden after finishing "Time Passes" and, in any case, it was almost done. In just a few more days, I'll have run through the entire stretch of this story about time and was far from having exhausted its treasures and traps. I would have to revise it all, then revise it again, but at least I will have cleared an initial path and sketched a first draft.

I wandered from booth to booth, looking at the colored fairy-tale figurines, Rapunzel, a life-sized farmer surrounded by her animals, or objects for sale, candles, various ornaments, amber, and there was mulled wine, potato pancakes with applesauce, from hut to hut—the booths were like miniature chalets—I heard people sharing their latest news with each other, I watched them warm themselves, meet before returning home in order to forget winter or prepare for Christmas. Did I feel my solitude more keenly here than elsewhere in the city? It was almost the opposite: I had the feeling that I too might meet someone I knew and chat a while before returning home. Home. How long had it been since I'd said that word, how long since I'd thought it? As a result of not saying words, we no longer think of them, they are thrown on the scrapheap, they pile up and become muddled, indistinguishable one from another. Living away from home—nowhere did I have a clearer sense of the effort, energy, and inner transformation this demanded than in this Christmas market. In the mirror, I was the same, but inside, after these weeks in Dresden? Near the last hut, where a girl had let down her golden braid so that someone could free her, I saw her. Or rather, I heard her voice, more exactly a call. The face of a soul. The silhouette of a friend. Something from the past.

We had only met in Paris. Although the overall horizon of our encounters was immense, geographically they were limited to a few streets. We had never gone together to most parts of Paris even though we often spoke of our travels. But we traveled separately, as if the point was to tell each other about them. In Dresden, I could have told her, there were fairy-tale characters, recognizable by a single detail—Rapunzel's braid, the goose girl's geese, obvious clues, but it was like entering a world of enchantment. I could have described to her the colors at dusk and taken pictures, as I sometimes had, to send to her. But there she was, in front of me, a sudden apparition. I like the fairy-tale world, too, she seemed to say, I need the reality of books to bear the world's reality and I try to bring the world into the books that I write, to capture its beauty, and its share of humanity and human suffering to incorporate them into my writing the way you add ingredients to a dish that has been simmering. I'll have to reread the books you wrote, I said to myself, I said to her, the books that became detached from you and now circulate, even more alone, more removed from the course of your life. Until then, I'd hesitated, I'd avoided opening her books, afraid of unexpectedly coming upon her face or the remains of a conversation. Reading a book by a recently deceased author is like crossing the threshold oneself or summoning the author back to life, like entering a space in which the living and the dead are indistinguishable; it is to move toward death and bring the dead closer to life. Those who ventured into the Underworld in Antiquity always came back shaken to the core: Orpheus unable to bring back Eurydice because he faltered at the last moment—and turned around—unable to take upon himself the absolute transgression; Aeneas taking the measure of the difference between a living person and a shade by trying to embrace his father—his arms embracing only emptiness. And yet a voice was guiding me and giving me a reason to go back, a reason to return home. I tried to imagine what I would be doing at that hour if I were in Paris, probably translating a few more lines of "Time Passes," then going out to shop. Surrounded by people who were getting together, I suddenly longed to see those close to me, longed for the sense of returning home, and besides, hadn't I already had an experience of fulfillment at the concert the other evening, after which I couldn't hope for anything better?

INTERLUDE

This is where the High Line ends. A large expanse, not long ago still empty and crossed by tracks on which not a single train ran. The space became filled with cranes, enormous pits, then an immense construction site near the station, while the trains now arrived at the former post office converted to a train station. This new neighborhood—Hudson Yards—emerged from the ground, more skyscrapers, more transparencies. Pointed shapes, sharp angles, slender towers. And a luxury shopping center. There are no more open spaces, no more wild vegetation, no more migratory birds. Everything is measured, monetized, studied. A site of capital, of investment, of consumption.

Tourists are already lining up to ascend the strange, rust-colored structure called the Vessel. Is it a space vessel? Although one that is anchored to the concrete slab, well anchored to reality?

The Hudson Yards was built above sea and flood levels. The air quality is measured, and sensors also measure noise pollution, and energy usage. Garbage is sorted, as is the recycling—waste is transported by pneumatic tubes. Restaurants, bars, boutiques—the commercial center spreads out its levels, its alleys, its escalators.

The ground reflects the lights of the shops and New York shines into its large plate-glass windows.

Nothing is missing, not even the alibi of art with the Shed. Part of the building—all transparence and horizontal lines—slips out of its sheath, retracts, expands, opens up, and closes. Moving, adjustable installations are layered over the eight levels, galleries, concert halls—nothing has been forgotten. Depending on the event, ticket prices range from ten to one hundred dollars.

VII

A veritable crowd reappears in "Time Passes" compared to the absence of humanity in the preceding pages.

George, Mrs. Bast's son, caught the rat, and cut the grass.

People we haven't encountered yet. Performing actions described in plain monosyllables. It's harder to keep to monosyllables in French. George, le fils de Mrs. Bast attrapait le rat et coupait l'herbe. There are no monosyllabic words in French for *caught* or *cut*.

They had the builders.

Il y avait les ouvriers, there were builders. But the impersonal doesn't account for the way *they* reinforces the sudden, overwhelming human presence, although also has an impersonal sense in English. Or it would have to be: ils avaient fait venir des ouvriers, they had the builders come, but in French that's too long, simply too long. And then we have the cadence of the next phrase.

Attended with the creaking of hinges and the screeching of bolts, the slamming and banging of damp-swollen woodwork, some rusty laborious birth seemed to be taking place, as the women, stooping, rising, groaning, singing, slapped and slammed, upstairs now, now down in the cellars. Oh, they said, the work!

Almost sound poetry, ingenious sounds following each other in a song of work, in concrete music, Vertov's *Dombas Symphony*. Aidée du grincement des gonds, du crissement des écrous, du battement et claquement de boiseries gonflées d'humidité, une laborieuse naissance rouillée semblait prendre place (or semblait se produire?), tandis que les femmes, penchées, relevées, en grognant, en chantant, battaient et balayaient, tantôt là-haut tantôt en bas dans les caves. Battaient and balayaient, beat and swept for slapped and slammed to keep the consonance. This passage appears in the manuscript in almost identical form, except that the *laborious birth* is announced at the beginning before it is replaced in later versions with the *attended*.

The sound of human labor and the pause for a well-earned tea break, contemplating the finished work. The fragility of destiny, of all human life subject to the outrages of time, dust, dirt, rust, and in the end, fragility vanquishes. Victory does not always go to the strongest.

Flopped on chairs they contemplated now the magnificent conquest over taps and bath; now the more arduous, more partial triumph over long rows of books, black as ravens once, now white-stained, breeding pale mushrooms and secreting furtive spiders.

The birds that flitted through the preceding pages have been relegated to the metaphorical. To be sure, there are mushrooms and spiders—the vegetable and animal kingdoms have not had their last words—but they are furtive and pale, merely transient and barely noticed. Mrs. McNab sees the old man walking across the lawn, talking to himself. He, who had never bothered to look at her. Whether this is a vision, a memory, or reality is not clear. Everything is described through the lens of a telescope, but the telescope too is a metaphor, an adjustment of vision, *in a ring of light*, which could be confused with the beam of the lighthouse. This scene is developed in much greater detail in the Berg manuscript, which states explicitly that he is a ghost. After this, memories connected to Mrs. Ramsay jostle each other and become more concrete. The Uniform edition, however, continues:

Some said he was dead; some said she was dead. Which was it? Mrs. Bast didn't know for certain either. The young gentleman was dead. That she was sure. She had read his name in the papers.

So she read newspapers then and therefore knew that there was a war and that people were dying in it. The two women converse, but we don't hear them. It's all narrated in reported speech, which increases the uncertainty. Although Mrs. McNab and Mrs. Bast have won the battle against time, nothing has been won in the stream of consciousness—impressions appear and disappear in the haze of existence.

—How do I translate *seascapes*? Paysage de mer?

—Two horizontal expanses in black and white, the sky and the sea, the sea and the sky. And then it turns to shades of gray, now light, now dark. Water and air.

—Baltic, Caribbean, Ligurian seas. Atlantic Ocean, Tyrrhenian Sea, Sea of Japan. Bay, cape, lake. Arctic, Tasmania, England, Open sea, enclosed sea.

—Nineteen-eighties or nineteen-nineties.

—And then, never any waves, just an undulation, a movement—calm and serenity.

—The horizon over the sea is the widest distance we can see, the photographer Hiroshi Sugimoto once observed when speaking about his works. Nothing stops our gaze where the sky meets the sea. And he added that the marine landscape is the only vision we have in common with prehistoric man.

Living somewhere temporarily, even if for an extended period, knowing you're not at home. Had I ever felt at home? Had I ever had the feeling of putting down my suitcase, of settling somewhere, or on returning to where I was living—a place to which I had the key, where I'd lived for years, an apartment I'd looked for and found but hadn't really invested myself in—did I ever say to myself, I'm home? Of course, compared to those who keep their possessions in a shopping cart, in plastic bags, in IKEA totes, to those who spend nights on a bench, in the street, under a tent provided by an NGO, I did have a home, a roof over my head. I'd been told that not so long ago, forty years maybe, train stations were open all night, but now they're locked to keep people who used to be called tramps and are now called homeless or unhoused from taking refuge there. This is as absurd and pointless as building a dike against the Pacific. The number of people sleeping rough has skyrocketed since then. I searched the Internet. For Paris Gare du Nord, for example, the first train leaves at 4:30 a.m. and the last at 1:00 a.m. Trains begin running again at 5:00 a.m. at Gare de l'Est and Gare de Lyon.

Paris . . . From Dresden, it seemed far away; nothing here recalled Paris, the histories of the two cities ran parallel, and I had the sense that I'd come from another world without knowing to what I could attribute that feeling. Basically, the only time I'd felt at home here was in the concert hall of the Kulturpalast, waiting for the concert to start and watching the audience arrive. There was that woman who had sat down next to me . . . The music, the *Coral de Caracola*. Listening to it—a quarter hour that extended well beyond any human measure of time—I had been one with myself. I was where I was, in pure presence, but paradoxically—or perhaps it was no paradox—listening demanded my complete attention, it drew me out of myself and into the music, it required that I forget everything I wasn't hearing, and yet, this moment of forgetting was precisely when I felt myself, when I felt at home.

Then comes the paragraph about the cook and life as it used to be. There were always people in the house, and often the washing up lasted long past midnight, Mrs. McNab assured Mrs. Bast (who hadn't known these times).

Ah, said Mrs. Bast, they'd find it changed.

Ah, dit Mrs. Bast, ils allaient la trouver changée. It, *la maison*, the house. But on reflection, maybe it would be better to say ils allaient trouver tout changé, they'd find everything changed, to preserve the sentence's neutrality. Mrs. Bast has become part of the household because it is her son George who is cutting the grass in the garden. And suddenly, this garden, which has been the scene of egregious events—giant artichokes among the roses—becomes nothing more than a plot overgrown with weeds, a chaos that has been returned to human dimensions.

She leant out of the window. She watched her son George scything the grass.

The transition from Mrs. Bast's words to her point of view is extraordinary. She only needs to lean out the window for the internal scene to become an external one. Briefly—the garden, the cut grass.

They might well ask, what had been done to it? Seeing how old Kennedy was supposed to have charge of it, and then his leg got so bad after he fell from the cart; and perhaps then no one for a year, or the better part of one; and then Davie Macdonald, and seeds might be sent, but who should say if they were ever planted? They'd find it changed.

Are we in Mrs. Bast's mind or in her conversation with Mrs. McNab? It doesn't matter much, actually. What is remarkable in this otherwise prosaic paragraph is the sudden accumulation of names. All the people who were supposed to take care of the house that we had seen abandoned and left at the mercy of the elements evolve in a parallel universe—or rather, it was the human race that was evolving in a parallel universe, that had left the planet like science-fiction characters fallen through a gap in time. This period had lasted more than a year, more than ten years, and now comes a return to the world and the world resumes its mundane, slightly tedious traits, full of superfluous details.

She watched her son scything. He was a great one for work—one of those quiet ones. Well they must be getting along with the cupboards, she supposed. They hauled themselves up.

Elle regardait son fils faucher l'herbe. Il travaillait très bien—et tranquillement. I stray too far from the original if I translate its simple words so literally, they get lost in a formulation that is much too complicated, much too long. Bon, il fallait s'occuper des armoires, supposait-elle. Elles se levèrent avec effort. Here it's the same. *Up* is translated with *avec effort*, or rather *up* is rendered with *levèrent* and *hauled* with *avec effort*. All this is too long. But the reflexive pronoun *se*, a single syllable, for *themselves* compensates somewhat for the length and in the end, the French sentence is hardly longer than the original. Now back to the preceding sentence: C'était quelqu'un qui travaillait très bien—et en restant calme. This is both a bit more removed and a bit closer . . .

Night was falling, had fallen. The season turned imperceptibly from autumn to winter, and even if winter had not yet officially arrived, it was making itself felt in the cold mornings, in the evenings that fell almost mid-afternoon, in the padded silhouettes of passersby swathed in several layers of clothing. I had finally decided that once I finished my translation of "Time Passes"—or rather a draft—I would leave. Leave, go back, go home: I wasn't lacking words, but I didn't know what they encompassed. I no longer saw Dresden as a city I wanted to immerse myself in to know better, or at least to apprehend it, but as a city I was going to leave. The time it takes to become attached to a place is the same as the time it takes to become detached. Isn't this absurd? Wouldn't it be better to stay home or merely pass through a place? To travel rather than seek to live elsewhere, as if another life were possible. To go from one city to another, to follow the coast, climb a mountain, to move on, to advance . . . I became lost in a labyrinth of sterile thoughts, simply to avoid opening the book and returning to the text, to not have to confront the void I was feeling, an emptiness at the thought of leaving, of ending the adventure that overwhelmed the relief of making a decision.

—Fleury, a village in eastern France with a mayor, a Zip code, and zero inhabitants.

—A village evacuated in 1916, at the beginning of the Verdun offensive, bombed, lost, and recaptured more than a dozen times successively by the French and Germans until the end of the war.

—The village was officially recognized as "Mort pour la France"—dead for France. No one lives there any longer, but a grateful fatherland has preserved its classification as a township. That's why it has a mayor.

—The entrance to the village, as with any other village in France, is marked with a sign bearing a name. Fleury-devant-Douaumont. But this sign stands in an empty landscape. There is not a single house on the horizon, just the road stretching past it.

—Woods on either side of the road.

—You have to leave the road, enter the woods, and walk along paths that follow the traces of old streets between the trees. Plaques recall the shops that once were there: the blacksmith, the cobbler, the school, city hall, and the street names.

—The village appears on Google Maps in a large green space in which only the memorial to the dead and the commemorative chapel are marked.

Before starting work in the morning, I would read the newspaper. A humanitarian ship, as those ships are called that roam the seas like the people they rescue, looking for host ports, which are as rare as the sight of a white whale, embarked on a venture as dangerous as Captain Ahab's quest. A German humanitarian ship had just rescued eighty-eight migrants, as we now say. France and Germany were willing to take sixty between them, Portugal five, and Ireland two. That made sixty-seven. That left twenty-one no country was willing to take. How would a selection be made? Another ship, an Italian one, had rescued a hundred and fifty people off the coast of Libya and transported them to Sicily. The numbers continued to pile up, people kept fleeing and the receiving countries, as they are called, accepted them reluctantly. Instead of looking for ways to cope with the increasing number of refugees—of whom the majority already were climate refugees—these countries sought ways to turn them away, to send them back to their countries of origin, to push them away. Like invaders. I read the newspaper. Compared to the reports of conflicts, uprisings, and large migration movements, the abandonment of a house on a Scottish island in the early twentieth century, was hardly significant. And yet it was. And yet this abandonment contained all the catastrophes of the last century and our current one. It was like—I searched the Internet, and it didn't take me long to find the Proust quote in *Swann's Way* about the memory released by a madeleine dipped into a cup of tea: "And just as the Japanese amuse themselves by filling a porcelain bowl with water and steeping in it little bits of paper which until then are without character or form, but, the moment they become wet, stretch themselves and bend, take on color and distinctive shape, become flowers or houses or people, permanent and recognizable . . . " Proust, the only writer Woolf read with anxiety, fearing she would find in his novels what she wanted to write. It was like those Japanese flowers, things at present invisible were taking shape within events.

Back to the text with, as a backdrop, the Christmas market that was starting to bustle, though it wouldn't reach the height of its glory until evening with its garlands of colored lights, its large Christmas tree, its Ferris wheel, its unsuspected sources of light on a gray day like this one when a soft rain troubled the view of the tramcars riding harmoniously on their rails.

At last, after days of labour within, of cutting and digging without, dusters were flicked from the windows, the windows were shut to, keys were turned all over the house; the front door was banged; it was finished.

Suddenly time and the rhythm accelerate. What had been presented as a thirteenth labor of Hercules is accomplished in just a few lines. True, the lines begin with *at last.* It's important to keep the passive voice because it preserves an atmosphere of times gone by, of that world abandoned by the human race, which foreshadowed what might be left after the prophesied apocalypse if it came—if the feather alight—if the Chernobyl exclusion zone were to expand. But the denuclearization machine had just been invented, the liquidators of this new battle were two cleaning women armed with their paltry implements, brooms and pails, dusters, and they were victorious.

Enfin, après le labeur à l'intérieur, les journées passées à creuser et couper à l'extérieur—no, the rhythm is off and as experience seems to prove, the sentences that are simplest at first glance are the hardest to translate. Enfin, après des jours de labeur à l'intérieur, de taillage et de bêchage à l'extérieur, des chiffons furent secoués par la fenêtre, les fenêtres refermées, des clés furent tournées dans toute la maison; la porte d'entrée claqua; c'était terminé. Enfin, après des jours (better than les journées) de labeur au-dedans, de taillage et bêchage au-dehors, des chiffons furent secoués par les fenêtres (because I had to use the same wording and so plural, not singular), les fenêtres refermées, les clés se tournèrent dans toute la maison; la porte d'entrée claqua; c'était fini (at first *fini* had struck me as too short, but on second thought it seems better than *terminé*—at least for now).

It was finished. That was certainly my feeling. There were roughly two pages left to translate—or rather, to untangle. I had to set my departure date and notify the hotel. Although I would have liked to see the market completely set up, I didn't want to spend Christmas here, to feel the season's inevitable familial ingathering and the unavoidable solitude if you aren't with your family or no longer have one. Christmas is the time when you have to be like everyone else, the time when you say to yourself, this year I'm not going to do anything, I'm not going to buy anything, I'll be far from my loved ones or I'll pretend I'm away, I'll stay home alone and act as if it were any another day, and at the last minute you surrender that glorious solitude and act like everyone else after all, relieved that you can, that you have the means to gather, you too, with your family—relieved that you have a family to gather with.

In the afternoon, contrary to my routine, I left my desk to go to the other side of the Elbe, to venture beyond the lively streets of Neustadt, which I knew, to explore areas I had never seen and, I liked to think, would not see again, only once, unknown in these streets, without memories or history, weightless. I passed buildings that looked alike, one after another, churches, a military academy, empty streets, a few green spaces, then came to a large white building with a vast esplanade, a building sliced into by a kind of pointed metal shard like a notch in the continuity of the classical architecture, disrupting the view, shocking. The building seemed to be waiting for those who approach, as I did, by the broad avenue whose perspective it ends, to climb the immense staircase of broad, flat steps. But I was alone and I advanced as if in a dream, in a kind of fluidity mixed with apprehension, a state of weightlessness. I entered despite the museum's off-putting subject—military history. Something seemed to be calling me in. There were no other visitors in the enormous, empty rooms and I wandered among uniforms and weapons, decorations and models, treaties and orders which recounted a history that, I felt, did not concern me.

I looked, lingered in front of a display of taxidermied animals that had served in military operations—an elephant, a dromedary, horses, a lion. War reached into all domains, mobilized all governments, all the arts, all the sciences, all means of transportation, ground, air, and water. The rusted fuselage of an airplane, masses of gleaming weapons, the menacing shape of a metal underwater monstrosity: I had a sense I was surveying the remains of a vanished civilization—which, no doubt, had found a way to contribute to its own demise—without knowing why I had been spared. The partition walls in the exhibition spaces resembled the hull of a submarine and this expedition through human violence assumed the contours of an undersea exploration or the journey to the center of the earth described by Jules Verne, with its large underground sea.

I walked along the aisles in the museum the way you walk through a cemetery. Of extinct species. Of past wars. In the room I was heading toward, I noticed a movement, a silent motion. I saw a silhouette. I kept walking without accelerating my pace, curious to see the visitor's face, to come across someone in the empty rooms of the museum, someone to greet. To say hello, nod, make some sign to show we belonged to the same world. Hopefully he or she won't be gone by the time I get to the room, I thought.

It was she—I realized I knew this before seeing her and that she was the one who had drawn me there, not the museum.

You took a while to get here, she said to me. We communicated silently, without using our voices.

I couldn't find you.

I was losing hope.

Can you lose hope where you are?

Everyone can lose hope.

You were looking for the sea . . .

Something else.

What?

If I knew, I wouldn't be looking.

What are you doing here? Why this place?

A public place, but one that is usually empty.

And then?

You'll leave.

How do you know?

I know.

Suppose I do leave.

I too have to leave. Do you understand?

I don't understand.

I thought not.

Tell me—why this place of death, why these empty rooms that evoke so much destruction . . .

I chose.

What is it you want to tell me?

Surrounded by weapons and shows of good will declaring peace.

You wanted?

To tell you that I have to leave.

I don't understand.

That you have to let me go.

I don't understand.

You have to stop thinking of me.

Why?

Each thought draws me back. And I, too, need to go away, to settle in another time, another world.

Each thought . . .

You think that I'm the one who called you, but you're the one who made me come. Each time it was you.

What was there in this room? A Don Quixote equipped with a gas mask on a mount consisting only of a saddle and a horse head also equipped with a gas mask. Don Quixote brandished a spear. The rest of the room was empty, like my soul and body. As if everything had left me, as if I were an empty envelope, with neither the recipient's name or address. In front of me were cannons pointed at an invisible enemy, sculptures of huddled figures seeking protection from rockets and bombs about to fall, animated images, static images, toys, and models paraded past—or was it I who marched past them? War and peace danced an endless round. I got lost, passing repeatedly through the same rooms under the impression that I was heading toward the exit—where was it? The concrete walls seemed to be closing in, would they trap me? Anything to keep from remembering that conversation—if you could even call it a conversation. Anything to keep from seeing her silhouette. I wanted to escape this place, this city, and get back to the text. I was right to shut myself up in my room, to take no other path but the one that led from my hotel to the café, to ignore the bridges and the river, the open spaces. To get back to the text, where order has finally returned.

And now as if the cleaning and the scrubbing and the scything and the mowing had drowned it there rose that half-heard melody, that intermittent music which the ear half catches but lets fall; a bark, a bleat; irregular, intermittent, yet somehow related; the hum of an insect, the tremor of cut grass, dissevered yet somehow belonging; the jar of a dorbeetle, the squeak of a wheel, loud, low, but mysteriously related; which the ear strains to bring together and is always on the verge of harmonizing but they are never quite heard, never fully harmonized, and at last, in the evening, one after another the sounds die out, and the harmony falters, and silence falls.

The sentence is long. I have to take a deep breath before diving in and heading for the other riverbank. Et maintenant, comme si le ménage, le nettoyage, le fauchage, le jardinage (Am I reading too much into it if I add jardinage, gardening? Is it too anodyne next to the chaos that must be overcome?) Or maybe the infinitive would be better than the substantive: Et maintenant, comme si nettoyer et frotter, faucher et tondre l'avaient noyée, maintenant s'élevait la mélodie à demi entendue, la musique intermittente que l'oreille perçoit mais qu'elle abandonne. And again, those monosyllables that are difficult to replicate in French. un aboiement, un bêlement—so much longer than *bark* and *bleat*. . . . aboiement, bêlement; irréguliers, intermittents et pourtant reliés; le bourdonnement d'un insecte, le tremblement de l'herbe coupée, séparée et faisant pourtant partie (this will have to be completely reworked) le choc d'un scarabée, le grincement d'une roue, fort, faible, mais mystérieusement reliés que l'oreille s'efforce de rassembler, est toujours sur le point d'harmoniser mais ils ne sont jamais totalement entendus, jamais pleinement harmonisés, et enfin le soir, les sons l'un après l'autre s'éteignent, l'harmonie vacille et le silence tombe. Or more directly: . . . mais on ne les entend jamais entièrement, jamais pleinement harmonisés, jusqu'à ce qu'enfin, dans le soir, l'un après l'autre les sons s'éteignent, l'harmonie vacille et le silence tombe.

A feeling of emptiness. I was in Dresden and Paris was calling me. My escape had been in vain, the city—my city—was telling me. Like all exiles and refugees, I had brought what I was fleeing with me—or at least its shadow. I who had often traveled, even in uncomfortable circumstances, had never stopped anywhere for an extended time like this, never tried to live elsewhere than at home, and these few weeks had brought me—along with solitude—an opening, a new perspective. And an awareness of how solid my ties were. Family, friends with whom I hadn't spoken, whom I'd answered with silence, they were the ones I longed to see. They were the ones calling me back.

Outside my window, the ginkgo I had watched change with the seasons and drip golden leaves was now bare and its black branches stood out in a ghostly pattern. The moon occasionally poured down its light; last night or two nights ago, the sky around it looked illuminated. It was a full moon—a perfect circle. But tonight there were only clouds, the invisible was taking over, was encircling me, whereas during the day everyone had seemed to be preparing for Christmas. The memory of my visit to the museum returned persistently, the weapons and armor, the sky filled with bombs as silent as dirigibles, but these images were merely the décor against which the scene I didn't want to think about and couldn't stop thinking about was playing. Everything I did was done to avoid it, and just as I had left Paris so that I would no longer be subject to sudden assault of memories, I wanted to leave Dresden to escape from the memory of the museum.

With the sunset sharpness was lost, and like mist rising, quiet rose, quiet spread, the wind settled; loosely the world shook itself down to sleep, darkly here without a light to it, save what came green suffused through leaves, or pale on white flowers by the window.

How I would have liked to experience the peace described here. Must peace always be won from peril—from chaos? Avec le coucher du soleil, la netteté se perdait, et comme le brouillard qui se lève, comme la brume qui se lève (brume for a shorter word than brouillard) le calme se levait, le calme s'étendait, le vent s'apaisait; avec nonchalance le monde se secouait pour s'endormir, dans une obscurité sans lumière, en dehors du vert (or would hormis le vert be better?) qui diffusait à travers les feuilles, ou les fleurs pâles et blanches à la fenêtre.

Vegetation has retreated to the backdrop again, reduced to a faint glow glimpsed at night, to a decorous window ornament. The peace of evening. As when, after a long walk, you see the lights of the first houses on the outskirts of a village or city, and tired but happy to have covered so many miles, crossed so many landscapes, you hope to find a hotel room. Quiet streets, little traffic and few passersby, several streetlights illuminating the pavement, old houses with closed shutters, everyone having already withdrawn to their homes but in the particular mindset of the hiker passing through, this withdrawal seems promising rather than hostile, a sign advertising a meal in a restaurant's quiet dining room, perhaps with a fire burning in the fireplace, where muted voices in conversation would presage the mists of dreamless sleep to come.

Au coucher du soleil se perdait la netteté, et telle la brume qui se levait, le calme s'élevait, s'étendait, et le vent s'apaisait; nonchalamment le monde se secouait pour s'endormir, dans une obscurité sans lumière à part le vert diffusé à travers le feuillage, la pâleur des fleurs blanches à la fenêtre. Or rather le monde s'ébrouait for *shook itself*? And *à part*, aside from, is not an attractive solution for *save*. Maybe *hormis*. Dans une obscurité sans lumière hormis le vert diffusé à travers le feuillage, la pâleur des fleurs blanches à la fenêtre. That's an improvement.

For the first time, I was working into the night, at the window, with complete darkness outside to make progress so that I could leave as soon as possible, or maybe just to keep my mind occupied. Absence kept digging into me—aren't you ever disappointed by the reception of your books, of how little response they receive sometimes? I'd asked her one day. I used to worry about it, she answered, but not anymore. I seem to remember that I asked this just before she was given a diagnosis for her fatigue. Time passes, once and for all, and we find ourselves on the other shore without knowing we had made the crossing. A plea was forming in me.

I need to talk to you, I thought with all my strength, I have to, one last time. Everything is raw.

No one in my room, no silhouette, no shade, no shape—I had turned out the light—I didn't see any movement, but I heard a voice. Someone. A breath.

What do you want? she said or I thought I heard her say.

I'd known, all day I'd known, but now that we were speaking, I no longer did. I felt nothing but an enormous void, like strokes of white paint covering the colors of the world. I wanted a farewell, some kind of conclusion.

Our conversations, I said, our discussions, I had the impression I was saying, missing—the words tumbled out, bumped into each without any logical sequence, without any particular meaning. My mind was empty or too full, everything was indistinguishable, nothing resurfaced after the shipwreck, sunken islands, churches fallen from cliffs, bridge-destroying windstorms, and instead of cities, a heap of destroyed buildings, postwar ruins.

What do you want? she said, or I thought I heard her say. Why did you call me?

I was sitting at the table in front of the window. Branches swayed outside. I don't know how to talk to you, I said, how to tell you how hard it is to get used to your absence.

That's not my concern.

What is your concern?

To detach myself—the process begins in the final days of your life, probably even earlier—and continues after. It's work.

Am I bothering you?

In a sense. We each have to go our own way. You're trying to find me whereas I'm trying to break away.

Where are you?

In an in-between. There are no words to describe it.

Does it last?

Time doesn't exist there, not like here, and space doesn't exist either.

I thought loss would be easier to bear elsewhere. This was true at the beginning, but . . .

I can't help you. I'm not the one to tell this to.

On the very last day . . .

It's gone.

On the last day, I talked to you. I'd like to know if you heard me . . .

There was no one—had someone been there? I was still sitting at the same table and had the feeling that I'd returned from a journey with no location, from a crossing. Far away, maybe the light of a lighthouse flashed, indicating a direction. We each had to go our own way, I knew this, I'd always known but now I had confirmation. This feeling of living my life almost as usual, followed by a kind of shadow that wasn't mine, or a look, would this feeling go away? The first days in Dresden, I was perfectly one with my life. Looking for a room, beginning the translation, exploring the city, all these concrete, quotidian activities required my full attention until one night, on the street near the high tower of a church, a silhouette came toward me.

[*Lily Briscoe had her bag carried up to the house late one evening in September. Mr. Carmichael came by the same train.*]

The brackets are back and they contain Lily Briscoe and Mr. Carmichael. Carmichael, the last of the company gathered around the Ramsays to disappear, who had stayed up late with Virgil before his light, his presence was extinguished.

Being there, being elsewhere, the words floated in space, without destination, they could turn against each other, had no meaning, barely a sound. Did I hear her voice, discern a presence, or simply populate my solitude? The last vision I had shied away from returned insistently—maybe the images of Dresden originated in it?

How could I sleep? I went out into the night and crossed the street to reach the river. Did I hope to see her one last time? I wished I had a flower to throw into the river, where the current would have carried it to the sea.

The color white everywhere, the bed, the walls, the face, the sheets. I saw them floating on the Elbe like a barque trying to reach the other shore, the final shore of the kingdom of the dead. In “Time Passes,” humans and the house escape universal death, even if some are gone, the human race has survived because the feather did not alight on the scale. Death had appeared in the white room, had weighed down the scale and taken someone, a presence, a friend. I had spoken, had said certain things, and I had the sense that she heard me even if her eyes were closed and she was gasping terribly—I won’t say, I won’t think the words usually used to describe these moments—even if she could not speak. An instant—so fleeting, I wasn’t sure it occurred—her breathing had calmed.

CODA

Then indeed peace had come. Messages of peace breathed from the sea to the shore.

What a beautiful way to indicate the war and the peace signed on the continent . . .

Never to break its sleep any more, to lull it rather more deeply to rest and whatever the dreamers dreamt holily, dreamt wisely, to confirm—what else was it murmuring—as Lily *Briscoe laid her head on the pillow in the clean room and heard the sea.*

Never to break its sleep, Virginia Woolf wrote in the middle of the 1920s, when the next war was not yet looming, when it was still possible to believe the last war would be the final one. The trauma was still vivid and initiatives to guarantee peace proliferated. Even the Great Depression was only a minute point on the horizon.

To believe again. To know that living means looking to the horizon, to the open, to hope.

Through the open window the voice of the beauty of the world came murmuring, too softly to hear exactly what it said—but what mattered if the meaning was plain?—entreating the sleepers (the house was full again; Mrs. Beckwith was staying here, also Mr. Carmichael), if they would not actually come down to the beach itself at least to lift the blind and look out.

In the Berg manuscript, the sea doesn't breathe the messages of peace, the waves do. Then the movement of the waves is described, forming the beginning of what would become several years later the magnificent novel, *The Waves*. Was the end of every book perhaps an announcement of the next? I wish I could have talked about this with my friend but, contrary to the *never any more* of the lighthouse, that end was final.

The beach, in the original version, is empty of human presence. Neither Lily Briscoe, nor Mr. Carmichael, much less Mrs. Beckwith appear on it. There is only the sound of the waves breaking on the shore.

They would see then night flowing down in purple; his head crowned; his scepter jewelled; and how in his eyes a child might look.

Mysterious allusions. A monarch and not a divinity of the night, an undivided dominion—the hope for a child, perhaps a new birth.

And if they still faltered (Lily was tired out with traveling and slept almost at once; but Mr. Carmichael read a book by candlelight), if they still said no, that it was vapour, this splendour of his, and the dew had more power than he, and they preferred sleeping; gently then without complaint, or argument, the voice would sing its song.

In the Berg manuscript, *his* refers to God, a strange apparition in Woolf's normally godless universe. The sky is not referred to as the heavens. But God disappeared from later versions and we have the sense that it's the night that is crowned and bearing a scepter, unless it is the lighthouse. That purple light, yes, it could be the lighthouse. Et s'ils hésitaient encore (Lily était épuisée du voyage et s'endormit presque aussitôt, mais Mr. Carmichael lisait un livre à la lumière de la bougie), s'ils disaient toujours non, que sa splendeur n'était que fumée—why not keep vapor, rather than smoke? Que sa splendeur n'était que vapeur, ou n'était que brume, que la rosée avait plus de pouvoir, qu'ils préféraient dormir; gentiment, sans se plaindre ni discuter, la voix chanterait sa chanson.

Lily and Mr. Carmichael have returned, the parenthetical is of a different kind. In the Berg manuscript, it's a vague, unspecified "we" that hears the voice.

Gently the waves would break (*Lily heard them in her sleep*); *tenderly the light fell* (*it seemed to come through her eyelids*).

In the Berg manuscript, the sentence reads *the wave breaks on the shore* after the storm, after the chaos, and this phrase will be taken up again in *The Waves* but in the past tense and put down as the closing words. Having written it, Virginia Woolf noted in her diary her relief at completing the task that had appeared to her at the end of *To the Lighthouse*: knowing how to capture her "vision of a fin rising on the wide blank sea."

And it all looked, Mr. Carmichael thought, shutting his book, falling asleep, much as it used to look years ago.

Again, we enter into someone's thoughts, again Mr. Carmichael is reading—Virgil still? As Sugimoto said, the sea is the only natural scenery that does not change over the years, decades, or centuries.

After so much crossing out, the final page of the Berg manuscript was written more or less in one rush. Still, the very end differs, ending with *the coming day*.

All the questions I didn't ask. How does the work advance? How does one version become another? How is the decision made to keep this passage rather than that one? Which divinity presides over the choice? Intellect? Intuition? Instinct? Was Mr. Carmichael reading the same book? Was everything as it used to be? Of course not, nothing is ever the same as before, there was that interlude, that rupture, something had happened—war, death, loss—and even if the lighthouse beam always swept over the same segment of the sea, different eyes were taking it in.

Indeed the voice might resume, as the curtains of dark wrapped themselves over the house, over Mrs. Beckwith, Mr. Carmichael, and Lily Briscoe so that they lay with several folds of blackness on their eyes, why not accept this, be content with this, acquiesce and resign?

Isn't this a message encouraging the acceptance of the human condition, to take things as they come? I had given notice for my room, I'd said I was leaving, and yet I didn't go, but turned back, returned to my room. I had a few lines left, one or two more days to spend in Dresden, a final visit to the Christmas market, one last look out of the café's large windows at the tramcars gliding past each other like ocean liners sailing to a distant destination.

The sigh of all the seas breaking in measure round the isles soothed them; the night wrapped them; nothing broke their sleep, until, the birds beginning and the dawn weaving their thin voices into its whiteness, a cart grinding, a dog somewhere barking, the sun lifted the curtains, broke the veil on their eyes, and Lily Briscoe stirring in her sleep clutched at her blankets as a faller clutches at the turf on the edge of a cliff.

I have never come across a better description of that indescribable sensation of being on the brink of falling at dawn in a state between sleep and waking, of being awake without knowing it, your heart faltering, an anxiety or loss burrowing into your consciousness.

Lily Briscoe has the last word as she will at the very end of the novel because is a painter, she is the artist, the creator. The consciousness keeping vigil.

Her eyes opened wide. Here she was again, she thought, sitting bolt upright in bed. Awake.

AFTERWORD

Translating Loss and Recovery

Cécile Wajsbrot is an accomplished and prolific writer with seventeen novels, a collection of short stories, and numerous essays to her name. She also translates from English and German into French. Her translations of Virginia Woolf, Jane Gardam, Arthur Conan Doyle, Charles Olson, Gerd Ledig, and Peter Kurzeck, among others, reflect the broad range of her interests and the breadth of her stylistic resources.

Wajsbrot was born in Paris in 1954 to Polish Jews. Her early writing uses the prism of her family's fate to examine the importance of memory, the presence of history in our private and public lives, the impact of silence within and between generations, and the precariousness of communication. Her later work increasingly focuses on the central role art and culture play in our lives. The recent collection *Haute Mer* (High Sea, 2022), is a five-novel cycle that explores various aspects of the ways in which art is created and received, spanning multiple genres and periods.

Wajsbrot's 2021 novel, *Nevermore*, interweaves these themes into a meditation on loss and recovery through the act of translation and its recuperative powers. An unnamed translator mourning the loss of a close friend retreats to Dresden to translate the "Time Passes" section of Virginia Woolf's *To the*

Lighthouse. Translating this lyrical evocation of time and its devastations in a city to which the writer has no connections and where neither her own language nor Woolf's are spoken offers her an interruption, a moment of suspension, that allows her to immerse herself more profoundly in this prose poem of ephemerality. The narrator delves into phrases from "Time Passes" and subjects them to the "inexact science and imperfect art" of translation. This, in turn, leads her to wide-ranging reflections on other instances of loss, destruction and reclamation including the Chernobyl disaster, the High Line in New York City, the bombing of Dresden and Wallmann's commemorative *Bell Requiem Dresden*, Arvo Pärt's use of tintinnabulation, the evacuation of the Hebridean island Hirta's inhabitants, Hiroshi Sugimoto's photographic series of seascapes, the Ville d'Ys, Debussy's *Cathédrale englouti*, and Ceri Richards's series of paintings by the same name, etc.

Individual sentences in "Time Passes," the ghostly corridor that links the first and third sections of *To the Lighthouse*, become springboards for meditations on the nature of memory and its relation to our present thoughts and experiences, on time's destruction and the destruction of time by man, on grief and mourning both personal loss and the cataclysmic losses of man-made disasters and wars. And yet, it is a novel shot through with hope and the possibility of renewal. Human consciousness and artistic creation are powerful counterforces to time's inevitable devastation.

Nevermore also embodies better than any work I've read the process of translation with all its hesitations and approximations, its dead ends and sudden illuminations, its gropings and fine polishing, its discouragements and delights. It is said that no one reads a text more closely than a translator, and Wajsbrot makes that experience of relentless and exacting attention accessible to all readers.

The greatest challenge in translating this novel is bringing to life the narrator's process of translating Woolf's prose into French as elegantly and convincingly as Wajsbrot does. For the particular difficulty of "translating Woolf into English," that is, of translating those passages that quote Woolf directly followed by French alternatives, I've devised several strategies that depend on the context and point being made:

(1) In the first strategy, I keep the Woolf sentences in italics and follow them with English alternatives that precisely echo the variations in French which the narrator is testing and rejecting. With this strategy I hope both to bring the process of translation alive for readers who have little or no access to the French and to draw all readers' attention to the beauties and idiosyncrasies of Woolf's style.

(2) My second strategy is to keep the narrator's variations in French in my text in a different font (Helvetica Neue Light). I translate them into English when a particular feature or conundrum of translation is being highlighted, for example, the discrepancies of verb tenses between languages and their failure to align perfectly. This strategy has the advantage of keeping the process of translation front and center in the reader's

mind and illustrating particular difficulties of translation in general and between French and English in particular. Readers who don't understand French can easily skip them without losing the thread of the narrator's arguments.

(3) In the third strategy, I have cut some of the narrator's more literal or less complicated French versions of Woolf's sentences in order to sharpen the focus on those alternatives that shed light on the process of translation. For example, Woolf's lines—*Were they allies? Were they enemies?*—do not pose significant or telling difficulties for translation into French. I therefore elided the French version, "Étaient-ils alliés? Étaient-ils ennemis?"

Another, more general, challenge is capturing the atmosphere of loss and melancholy without heaviness or sentimentality. The narrator's dead friend is a ghostly but strong presence in Dresden and the vast legacy of historical and personal loss this presence evokes provides a particularly poignant backdrop to the narrator's grieving.

As is clear from the many musical references and themes and the cadences of her prose, Wajsbrot has an ear that is finely attuned to rhythm. I have striven to capture those cadences in English, sometimes using different beats and measures but always with an ear to equal internal consistency and beauty.

***

I would like to thank Cécile Wajsbrot and Anne Weber for their encouragement and advice and Alice McCrum, the former Programs Manager at the American Library in Paris, for her early enthusiasm for *Nevermore* in multiple languages.

Tess Lewis
New York, April 2024

SOURCES

Aeneid, Virgil, translated by John Dryden.

Baku: Symphony of Sirens. Arseny Avraamov, in *Sound Experiments in the Russian Avant Garde, 1908–1942.* Recommended Records, 2009.

Bucolics, Aeneid and Georgics of Virgil (J. B. Greenough trans.). Ginn & Co., 1900.

The Bells. Rachmaninoff, orchestra and choir of the Philharmonie du COGE. Directed by Jordan Gudefin (orchestra) and Frédéric Pineau (choir). Performed at the Paris Philharmonic, 2 June 2018.

Cantus in Memorium Benjamin Britten. Arvo Pärt. Proms 2010 BBC Symphony Orchestra. Directed by Edward Gardner.

La Cathédrale engloutie. Prelude by Debussy. Played by Debussy in *Masters of the Piano Rolls*, Dal Sagno, 2004.

La Cathédrale engloutie. Series of paintings by Ceri Richards at the Tate Gallery.

Chernobyl. Five-episode mini-series written by Gray Mazin and directed by Johan Reck.

The Edge of the World. Michael Powell, 1937. Available on Daily Motion.

Glocken Requiem. Heinrich Johannes Wallmann. Available at: https://bit.ly/-3Rsweog

Le Haut Livre du Graal: Perlesvaus (Armand Strubel ed. and trans.) *Lettres gothiques.* Le Livre de Poche, 2007.

L'Homme qui rit. Victor Hugo. Garnier-Flammarion, 1982.

Hebrides Overture. Felix Mendelssohn. London Symphony Orchestra. Directed by Claudio Abbado, 1988.

Organ Music. Juan Allende-Blin, Cybele records, 2005.

On the Highline. Annick La Farge. Thames & Hudson, 2014.

The Phantom Light. Michael Powell. 1935.

Seascapes. S series of photographs by Hiroshi Sugimoto.

Streit um Kirchenglocken. Ddocumentary by Ulrike Lefherz, 2019, along with various articles on the bell cemeteries.

Swann's Way. Marcel Proust (C. K. Scott Moncrieff and Terence Kilmartin trans). Modern Library, 2004.

Symphonie fantastique. Hector Berlioz. Chicago Symphony Orchestra. Directed by Claudio Abbado. Deutsche Gramophone, 1984.

Chernobyl: A Natural History. Documentary by Luc Riolon, 2010.

To the Lighthouse. Virginia Woolf. Harcourt, Inc. 1927.

Graves Without Names. Rithy Panh, 2018.

Walden, Henry David Thoreau. Penguin Classics, 1986.

War Requiem. Benjamin Britten, Galina Vishnevskaya, Peter Pears, Dietrich Fischer-Diskau. London Symphony Orchestra. Directed by Benjamin Britten. Decca, 1963; remastered 1999.

Woolf Online. Digital archive of *To the Lighthouse* created in 2013. See http://www.woolfonline.com